Enid Blyton

A Second Book of
Naughty Children

*Illustrated by
Kathleen Gell*

GW00728134

ARMADA

First published in Great Britain in 1947
by Methuen & Co. Ltd.

Daddy's Best Knife and *Ronnie Gets
a Shock* first published as part of
A Book of Naughty Children
in 1944 by Methuen & Co. Ltd.

Republished by Dragon Books 1971
This Armada edition 1989

Armada is an imprint of the Children's Division,
part of the Collins Publishing Group,
8 Grafton Street, London W1X 3LA

Printed and bound in Great Britain by
William Collins Sons & Co. Ltd, Glasgow

CONTENTS

'Go away dear, I'm busy'

THE BOY WHO BROKE HIS PROMISES

Albert was the boy who broke his promises. He was such a nice boy to look at, his eyes were so bright and his smile so merry – and yet nobody could trust him!

'I'll do my homework as soon as I finish my tea,' he promised his mother each day. But after tea he ran off to play, and forgot all about his homework.

'I'll never bite my nails again!' he promised his teacher, when she said how dreadful his bitten nails were. But the very next minute his fingers were in his mouth, and he was nibbling at his poor, ugly nails!

'I'll put away my toys and not leave one out,' he told his aunt when she came to look after him one day. But he forgot, and his promise was broken.

'Albert, promises are made to be kept and not to be broken,' his mother said. 'What is the use of making promises you never keep? People will not trust you.'

'Oh, I always *mean* to keep my promises,' said Albert. 'But I forget.'

His mother was worried. She didn't want him to grow up into somebody that could not be trusted to keep his word. So she told his old Great-Aunt, and Aunt Jenkins nodded her snow-white head.

'Send him to me for a few days,' she said. 'I'll cure him for you!'

So Albert's bag was packed and he set off in the bus to Aunt Jenkins. He had never been to her house before, but he knew her very well, because she often came to his mother's house, and she always brought him a present.

Great-Aunt Jenkins was pleased to see him. She took him upstairs to his little bedroom. It was very cosy.

'I hope you'll try and keep your room tidy for me,' she said.

'Oh, yes, I promise it will always be as neat as can be,' said Albert. But as soon as Great-Aunt had gone out of the room he tipped his bag up, and out fell everything at once! And there Albert left them. He just simply couldn't be trusted to keep his word about anything!

He went downstairs. 'What's for tea, Great-Aunt?' he said.

'Well, how would you like buns with jam and cream inside, and chocolate cake with walnuts on top?' asked Great-Aunt.

'Ooooh!' said Albert. 'Do let's!'

'Very well, I'll get them,' said Great-Aunt. So Albert longed and longed for tea-time, and rushed into the dining-room when the tea-bell went.

But do you know, there was only bread and butter and plain biscuits on the table! No buns – and no cake at all.

'Oh, Great-Aunt! Where are the jammy buns with cream, and the chocolate cake with walnuts that you promised?' asked Albert.

'Dear me, I quite forgot about them,' said Great-Aunt.

'But, Great-Aunt, you promised, and promises shouldn't be broken,' said Albert, almost crying.

'That's so,' said the old lady. 'But still, you promised to keep your room neat for me, Albert, and it is in a dreadful mess. So as you broke *your* promise, perhaps you won't mind me breaking mine. Now, hurry up and eat your bread and butter.'

'Great-Aunt, may I stay up till eight o'clock tonight?' said Albert, who usually went to bed at seven.

'Yes, if you like,' promised Great-Aunt. 'It will be a treat for you! Get my scissors after tea, Albert, and go and snip all the dead flowers off in the front garden for me, will you? There are such a lot, and I shall be too busy to do them today.'

'Yes, I will, Great-Aunt,' promised Albert. But after tea he wandered down to the field at the bottom of the garden, and played at Red Indians there, crawling in and out of the hedge, and yelling loudly whenever he saw the dog next door. The dog was supposed to be an enemy Indian.

'Oh, bother!' he said to himself, when he remembered that he had said he would snip off the dead flowers for Great-Aunt Jenkins. 'It's a nuisance to stop my play. I'll do Aunt's job tomorrow.'

Suddenly the bell rang to call him indoors. Albert went. Great-Aunt was upstairs.

'Bed-time,' she called. 'Hurry up, because I have to go out soon and I want you in bed first.'

'But, Great-Aunt, you promised I could stay up till eight o'clock!' said Albert. 'It's only seven!'

'Oh, well, I've changed my mind,' said Great-Aunt. 'And you changed yours about snipping off the dead flowers for me, so that makes us even! You broke your promise and I broke mine! Hurry now, and don't look so miserable. I'll give you a sweet orange when you're in bed. Remember to wash yourself well, won't you? I have run the water in the bath.'

'Yes, Great-Aunt,' said Albert gloomily, and he got undressed. He got into the nice hot bath but he didn't bother about washing, and suddenly he heard his Great-Aunt's voice from downstairs.

'Are you in bed yet?'

'Nearly!' shouted Albert, jumping out of the bath and dragging on his pyjamas without drying himself! He brushed his hair and jumped

8

into bed. His Great-Aunt came in.

'Have you brought my nice juicy orange that you promised me?' asked Albert.

'Oh, bother! No, I haven't!' said Great-Aunt. 'Never mind, you can have it tomorrow.'

'But you promised I could have it now!' said Albert, thinking that really Great-Aunt couldn't be trusted at all!

'Well, *you* promised to wash yourself well in the bath, and as far as I can see your face is still as dirty as when I left you, and your hands are quite black,' said Great-Aunt. 'I expect if I looked at your knees they would be just as bad. So you can't blame me if *I* don't keep my promises, Albert. Perhaps I should be a bit more particular about it if you kept *yours*.'

The next day was just as bad. Great-Aunt promised all sorts of wonderful things, and Albert felt most excited when he heard them.

'There's a circus coming this afternoon,' said his Great-Aunt. 'We might go to see it. I think it is in the field near by. Oh, and what would you like for dinner? Would you like an ice-cream pudding?'

'Oh, yes!' said Albert, who liked ice-cream better than anything else. 'And, Great-Aunt, would you get out that lovely bow-and-arrows that belonged to Great-Uncle years ago? I'd love to play with the bow.'

'Yes, I'll get it out this morning,' said Great-Aunt. 'That's a promise!'

Well, it may have been a promise, but Great-Aunt Jenkins didn't keep it! When Albert went to ask for the bow-and-arrows, she was busy cooking in the kitchen.

'Go away, dear, I'm busy!' she said. 'I haven't bothered about the bow this morning. I don't know where it is.'

'But, Great-Aunt, you did promise!' cried Albert.

'And who promised to make his bed this morning and didn't?' said Great-Aunt. 'And who promised to fetch me the eggs from the hen-house and didn't? And who promised to fill the bird-bath with water and didn't?'

Albert went red. Had he really made all those promises and broken them? Well, then, he really couldn't blame Great-Aunt for doing as *he* did. He went out without another word.

At dinner-time he ate his meat and potatoes and gravy eagerly, hoping that the ice-cream pudding would be very large indeed. But do you know, there was only a small rice pudding and nothing else!

'Great-Aunt! You've broken your promise again!' cried Albert. 'You said we'd have ice-cream pudding!'

'Did I really?' said Great-Aunt. 'Oh, well, I forgot. I suppose you forgot to change your shoes when you came in, Albert? You promised you would change them, but I see there is mud on the carpet. And I believe you said you would wash your hands. Well, well – you forgot, and I forgot. So we won't blame each other, will we?'

Albert went red. He ate his rice pudding without a word. All the time he ate it he was thinking about the circus. Would Great-Aunt keep her promise about that? He hardly dared to ask her. If only, only she would!

Well, she didn't! When Albert went to remind her at half-past two, she was in her bedroom, having a rest on her bed. She was quite cross at being disturbed.

'Circus! Who said anything about a circus?' she cried. 'I may have promised to take you this morning, but I've changed my mind this afternoon. I'm tired and I want a rest. Go away.'

'But, Great-Aunt, you really did promise!' said Albert, and burst into tears.

'Come here, Albert,' said Great-Aunt in a funny sort of voice. So Albert went and stood beside her.

'Albert, do you like me when I break my promises?' said Great-Aunt. 'Do you trust me any more?'

'No,' said Albert. 'I don't feel as if I do trust you, Great-Aunt. And I don't like you at all when you break your word. It makes me feel so disappointed and angry.'

'Well, you know, Albert, I've just been doing it to show you what people think of *you* and feel about *you* when you keep promising things and forgetting them,' said Great-Aunt. 'It's horrid,

11

isn't it? It's quite enough to make people cry and feel cross. That is how you make people feel, too, when you break *your* promises, Albert.'

'Great-Aunt, I will really try now to keep my promises – all of them,' promised Albert. 'I didn't know how horrid I made people feel when I broke them. I won't do it again.'

'Well, you'll find it difficult at first,' said Great-Aunt. 'But you must keep on trying. Now, will you promise me to weed that untidy bit of garden this afternoon, and to wash your hands for tea, and change your muddy shoes?'

'Yes, Great-Aunt,' said Albert.

'And *I* will promise you jammy, creamy buns for tea again, and chocolate cake with walnuts, and the circus tonight!' said Great-Aunt. 'We will see how we can manage to keep our promises!'

Well, Albert weeded the garden, and washed his hands, and changed his shoes – and sure enough there were jammy, creamy buns for tea, and chocolate cake, and they went to the circus that night! It was lovely!

Albert kept his promises next day too, and there was ice-cream pudding for dinner, and he was allowed to play with the wonderful bow-and-arrows all morning! He went to bed at eight o'clock for a treat, and had a juicy orange.

He was quite sorry to go home. But, dear me, how surprised his mother was to find Albert so changed! If he said he would do a thing, he did it. If he promised he wouldn't, he didn't.

'Why Albert, I really believe you are to be trusted after all!' said his mother. And so he was. But he never told her how Great-Aunt Jenkins had cured him. He was rather ashamed of that!

I am sure you keep *your* promises – but if you know anyone who doesn't, send them along to Great-Aunt Jenkins. She'll soon cure them!

MATILDA SCREAMS THE HOUSE DOWN

There was once a little girl who screamed whenever things went wrong. My goodness, how she screamed! She made everybody jump, and the cat and dog flew behind the sofa in fright. The people next door shut their windows, and passers-by wondered whatever was the matter.

'I don't know what to do with Matilda!' said her mother. 'If I smack her for screaming, she only screams more loudly! If I take no notice at all, she screams until I do! And if I give her what she is screaming for, she makes up her mind to scream next time. Oh dear, oh dear!'

Now one day, when Matilda was screaming, a little band of brownies passed by. When they heard the dreadful screams their hair stood on end, and they trembled with fright. Then one of them peeped in at the window and saw that it was only Matilda, sitting on the floor kicking her heels on the carpet, screaming for all she was worth!

'I want ice-cream!' screamed Matilda, and she yelled and howled till the cat jumped up the chimney in fright.

'You naughty girl!' said Bron, the chief brownie, looking in at the window. 'You very naughty girl! You'll scream the place down one day!'

Matilda looked at him angrily. 'I wish I could,' she said. 'I'd like to scream the house down. Then perhaps my mummy would give me a strawberry ice-cream.'

Bron turned to his little men. 'She says she'd like to scream the place down,' he said, with a grin. 'Shall we take her to Tumble-down Land and let her try?'

'Yes!' they shouted, putting their hands over their ears, for Matilda had started again. Into the house they swarmed, caught hold of Matilda by the hair, the hands and her dress, and hurried her, still screaming, out of the window. Matilda was most surprised. She struggled. She wriggled. It was no good at all. She simply *had* to go with those little brownies!

They hurried her down the road and into a lane she never remembered seeing before. Into a wood she went and out at the other side – and there she was, in funny Tumble-down Land!

There were strange-looking houses everywhere, all crooked and leaning over as if they must fall at any moment. There were sheds just hanging together by a few nails. It was a funny-looking place.

'Now, Matilda,' said Bron pleasantly, 'you can scream the place down. Go into this house to begin with.'

15

He took her into a tumble-down place, and the little men sat her on the floor with a bump. Matilda was very angry indeed. She opened her big mouth and screamed at the top of her voice. My, how she screamed!

And she screamed the place down – yes, she really did! The whole house came tumbling down round her with a crash and bang! My goodness, Matilda was startled! She stopped screaming for a moment and looked at all the mess. A bit of brick hit her on her head and hurt her. She screamed again. Down fell another bit of the house, and soon it was all in pieces around her, and dust flying about everywhere! Matilda was really frightened.

Bron peeped round the mess. 'Good!' he said. 'You screamed that place down beautifully, didn't you! Now come and do another.'

Poor Matilda was dragged into an old smelly shed and dumped on the floor again. She was very angry, so she opened her mouth and let out such a piercing yell that even the brownies jumped in alarm.

Down fell the shed at once! Not a bit of it was left! A small board fell on Matilda's leg and she screamed in pain. The brownies pulled her up at once.

'Don't waste your screams,' they said. 'This is fun to watch. Come and scream another place down!'

And into a bigger house they pushed the

Matilda had started again

angry little girl, still yelling and screaming. The house began to fall down at once! Matilda was afraid she would be hurt and tried to get out – but the brownies pushed her back.

'No, don't come out yet,' they said. 'You haven't screamed the place down, Matilda. Scream!'

'I shan't,' said the little girl, and she shut her mouth firmly.

'Your mother won't give you ice-creams,' said Bron suddenly, and of course Matilda at once screamed in anger, and down came the house, crash-smash-bang-clang! Matilda rushed out in fright, and she actually remembered that she had better not scream in case she brought down a chimney on top of her!

'Take me home – oh, take me home!' begged Matilda. 'I don't like this. I don't like screaming the place down.'

'Well, if you're sure you're not going to scream any more just now, I suppose the fun is over,' said Bron. 'But look here, Matilda, we'll be along the next time you scream, and we'll let you scream a few more places down for us. It's such fun to watch!'

Matilda pursed up her mouth and didn't say a word. If those little men thought she was going to scream any more places down for them, they were mistaken, Matilda thought to herself. Good gracious! She might have been badly hurt!

She was taken home. Her mother popped her

head in the room and saw Matilda playing quietly with her toys. 'I'm just going out to the town,' she said to Matilda. 'I won't be long.'

'I want to come too,' said Matilda. But her mother said no. Matilda was just going to open her mouth and scream when she remembered those little men. She shut her mouth firmly. She was not going to scream any more places down – and, dear me, how dreadful it would be if she screamed her own house down round her ears! That would never do!

Her mother was surprised that Matilda didn't scream as usual – but she was even more surprised as the days went by and Matilda screamed no more. How pleased everybody was – but nobody knew why Matilda was suddenly so good.

But I know and so do you! And if you know a screamer, just given them this story to read, will you? It would be fun to take them to Tumble-down Land and see them screaming a few houses down round their heads, wouldn't it?

THE STRANGE BLUE SWEETS

Once upon a time there was a small boy called Ned. He went to school with all the other children, and he would have liked it very much indeed if three other boys had not been so horrid.

They were Tom, Kenneth, and Denis. Tom was a very big boy for his age, and he loved teasing the other children, who were not so strong and big as he was.

Kenneth was a horrid little boy, who loved to pinch the children next to him. And when they squealed out he always said that he hadn't pinched them. He had such a nice little face that his teacher always believed him, so he was never punished.

Denis was just as horrid as the other two, but in a different way. He would kick people's ankles whenever he could, and this hurt the other boys and girls very much.

The worst of it was that nobody dared pinch or kick back, because the three bad boys always went about together, and no one dared to fight the three of them.

'It's too bad!' Ned said to the others. 'We just can't do anything. It's no good telling tales

– that's just the way to make teacher cross with *us*, because she hates tale-tellers. And we can't pinch or kick or tease those boys because if we do they'll only treat us all the more badly. I really don't know what to do.'

Now Ned had a great friend. She was the old balloon-woman who sold red, yellow, green and blue balloons at the corner of his street. Ned often bought a balloon from her, and he used to talk to her a lot, telling her all about school and his cat at home, and how his mother could make the best chocolate cakes in the world.

One day Ned had a bruise on his leg, and the old balloon-woman saw it. 'How did you get that?' she said.

'Oh, Kenneth did that,' said Ned. 'He's always doing it. And Tom is just as bad, because he is so big he can tease the children all playtime. He pulls the girls' hair, and fights the boys. Then there is Denis. He likes to kick our ankles, and if we try to kick him back he tells Tom, and Tom fights us again. School would be lovely if it wasn't for those three horrid boys.'

'Dear me!' said the old balloon-woman, and she looked quite worried, because she was fond of Ned. 'I wonder if I can help you. Come back this afternoon and I will give you something that *may* help you.'

So Ned went to see her again that afternoon, and she gave him a round pill-box. Inside were three blue sweets, the queerest Ned had ever seen, because they spun round and round in the box as if they were alive.

'My old Granny used to make these sweets,' said the balloon-woman. 'They do queer things. When you are in trouble with any of those bad boys, just pop one into your mouth and see what happens! Good luck to you, Ned!'

Ned thanked her and ran off with the sweets, feeling rather excited. He had always thought that the balloon-woman was a bit magic, and now he knew she was!

He put the box of sweets into his pocket. 'They may come in very useful,' he said to himself. 'I wonder what will happen when I suck them!'

He found out the very next day! It was playtime and all the children were out in the playground. The two teachers were indoors, correcting books. Tom thought he would have a fine game at pulling the girls' hair and hitting the boys smaller than himself.

'Stop that!' suddenly shouted Ned, and he went up to Tom.

'Ho, ho!' said Tom, quite surprised. 'You are very bold all of a sudden, Ned!'

He slapped Ned hard on the cheek with his hand. The little boy was angry. He slipped one of the strange blue sweets into his mouth and waited to see if anything would happen.

And something *did* happen! Ned suddenly grew to twice his size! It was most peculiar!

There he was as large as a man, standing high above Tom, who looked as astonished and as scared as could be.

'If you slap me, it is only fair to let me slap *you*!' said Ned, in a strange, loud voice. 'I think that what you need is a very, very good spanking!'

And, dear me, he picked up Tom and gave him the best spanking that naughty boy had ever had in his life!

'There!' said Ned to all the surprised and delighted children. 'That has taught him what it feels like to be spanked and slapped. Would you like to slap anyone else, Tom? If you would, just say so, and you can. And then, in return, I will spank *you* again. We will play a fine spanking game!'

'Oh, no, no!' wept Tom, who was really frightened. He was not at all a brave boy, really. It was only because he was so big that he had dared to tease the others. He ran away to a corner and stood there by himself, crying hard.

Ned smiled. Ah! It was fine to be able to show a bad boy like Tom just what it felt like to be teased. Perhaps Tom would be better in future.

He had been sucking the blue sweet – and now the last of it slid down his throat. At once Ned slipped back again to his own small size. The school bell rang, and he ran in with the others. Everybody was excited, and they stared at Ned as if they couldn't understand him at all. And indeed it was a very strange happening!

It was dictation. Kenneth, the boy who loved pinching people, was very good at this. He wrote his words down quickly, and then stared round, bored, wondering who to pinch. Good! There was fat little Fanny in front of him. He would pinch her and make her squeal! So he bent forward when the teacher was not looking and pinched poor Fanny hard.

'Ooooooh!' squealed Fanny. The teacher looked up angrily. 'Be quiet, Fanny,' she said. Fanny bent over her work with tears running down her cheeks. Ned looked at her, and felt sorry. She was a dear little girl, and it was a shame to see her hurt.

He opened his pill-box, took out the second of the strange blue sweets, and put it into his mouth. He began to suck it. What would happen now?

Well, a very queer thing happened! Ned's right arm grew enormously long, and so did his fingers and thumb! It grew so long that he could send his hand under three desks and three chairs, and reach right to the back of the room to where that horrid Kenneth was sitting, grinning to himself because he had made poor Fanny squeal.

Ned's long fingers came to Kenneth's plump leg. Ha, ha! Kenneth, there's a shock coming to you! What a pinch Ned's long fingers gave that plump leg!

'oooooooOOOOOOH!' yelled Kenneth, jumping out of his seat. He saw Ned's long hand and arm going quickly back underneath the desks and chairs, and he stared in fright.

'Kenneth! How dare you make that noise!' said the teacher sharply.

'Ned pinched me! He pinched my leg hard!' wept Kenneth, who wasn't at all brave.

'How can you tell such a naughty story!' scolded the teacher. 'Why, Ned is right in the front of the class, and you are at the back. He couldn't possibly reach. Go and sit by yourself in the corner there. I won't have you squealing like that, and telling stories.'

So Kenneth had to take his pencil and book right away to a corner by himself. But Ned's long arm could reach right over to the corner! And under the desks and chairs it went again, over the floor, right to Kenneth.

Pinch! Kenneth's arm was held hard by Ned's long fingers and pinched.

'OooooOOOOH!' squealed Kenneth again. 'Ned's pinching me!'

But by the time the teacher looked up, Ned's long strange arm had gone back again!

'Kenneth! How can you say such a thing when you are in that corner far away from everyone!' said the teacher, really cross now. 'You will lose your next playtime for being so naughty!'

Kenneth began to cry again. All the children

25

looked at one another in astonishment, because they had seen Ned's long arm. My goodness! What a good punishment for unkind Kenneth!

The blue sweet disappeared down Ned's throat. His arm went back to its right size again. The little boy wondered what the third sweet would do. Really, this was great fun! Nobody had been able to punish the unkind boys before.

Well, the third sweet came in very useful indeed. When they were standing in line, singing, Denis suddenly decided to do a little kicking. So he kicked hard at Mary, the little girl next to him. His shoe hit her on her ankle, and she squeaked in pain. Then Denis kicked the boy in front of him. The teacher didn't hear the squeaks and squeals because the children were singing.

But Ned had seen what Denis was doing, and quickly he popped the third blue sweet into his mouth. And what do you suppose happened *this* time? Why, his right leg and foot grew long, just as his arm had done! And the long leg wound in and out of the line of girls and boys until it reached Denis.

Kick! Ned's shoe kicked Denis hard on the ankle and the naughty little boy cried out sharply. The teacher stopped playing the piano and looked round.

'Who made that noise?' she said.

'I did,' said Denis. 'Somebody kicked me.'

'Well, really, I don't know what is happening

to you all this morning,' said the teacher. 'Denis, come and stand out here by me. Then no one can kick you.'

So Denis went and stood out in the front of the class, by the piano. But Ned's foot was quite long enough to reach him there! Goodness, you should have seen it, wriggling all round the piano so that the teacher wouldn't see it – and reaching Denis, to kick him sharply on the ankle!

'Ow, ooh, ow!' yelled Denis. The teacher nearly fell off the piano-stool in fright.

'Denis! How dare you!' she cried.

'Somebody kicked me!' wept Denis, rubbing his ankle.

'How can you say that, when you are standing by *me*, right away from everybody,' said the teacher. 'Go out of the room. And if I have any more trouble this morning you will all lose your next holiday.'

Ned's leg went back to its right size as soon as he had eaten the sweet. But, dear me, how the children giggled when they remembered all the queer things that had happened to Ned that morning!

The next playtime Ned beckoned everyone to him – Tom, Kenneth, and Denis as well.

'Now listen to me,' he said. 'We've had enough of hitting and kicking and pinching in this school. It is much nicer to be kind. But if anyone begins being horrid again – well, LOOK

27

OUT FOR ME, that's all!'

And after that the three horrid boys never dared to tease any of the smaller ones again, but were as polite and nice as could be. As for the old balloon-woman, she laughed so much when she heard Ned's story that she let her balloon-strings go, and very nearly lost them all!

'What a joke!' she said. 'Oh, how I wish I'd been there when you sucked those three strange sweets, Ned!'

I wish I'd been there too, don't you?

A SHOCK FOR JAMES!

Auntie Jane had given Mother a lovely pot of clear golden honey. Her bees had made it the summer before, and she was very proud of it.

'Can I have some of it, Mother?' asked James.

'Yes, but not until tea-time,' said Mother. 'You had marmalade for breakfast, and there is a jam pudding for dinner; you must wait for your honey.'

But do you know, James couldn't possibly wait! He watched to see where Mother put the honey – and the jar went into the larder, on the top shelf, where jams and bottled fruits were kept.

James went out to play after dinner, but he kept thinking of that honey! If only he could have just a taste! Just a little teeny-weeny taste, off the end of his finger!

Well, if you think and think of things like that, you want them so much that you can't stop yourself from having them! So it wasn't very long before James found his legs walking to the kitchen door.

'I wonder where Mother is!' he thought. He peeped in at the door. Mother wasn't there. She was upstairs putting on her new frock. James slid inside the door and looked at the larder door opposite. It was fast shut.

His legs took him to the larder. His hands opened the door, though all the time his mind was saying, 'I shouldn't do this! I shouldn't do this!'

He got into the larder. He looked up at the shelf. It was too high to reach! He didn't like to get a chair in case he made a noise and Mother came down to see what he was doing.

'If I go outside and stand on the box there, and push the window open, I believe I can just get my arm along the shelf and reach that honey!' thought James. So he shut the larder door and ran outside. He stood on the box there, and pushed at the larder window. It slid open.

James put in his arm – yes, he could just reach nicely along the shelf! He got hold of the honey-pot and took off the lid. He dipped his finger into the honey; my word, it *was* good! He dipped in again, and licked – and again.

A little honey-bee came flying by, and smelt the honey. It flew in at the window at once, and buzzed round the honey-pot.

'Go away, bee, go away!' said James crossly. He dipped his finger into the pot again and was just going to lick it when the bee flew straight on to it! James very nearly put the bee into his mouth!

He was so frightened that he hit at the bee with the honey-pot, which was in his left hand.

The pot struck against the window-sill and broke! Honey poured all over James's hand and arm, and some went on his jersey.

The bee flew off to tell its friends all about the lovely honey. James jumped down off the box in fright. Now what would Mother say? He would throw the broken pot on to the rubbish-heap, wash himself, and say nothing. Wasn't he a bad little boy?

But before he could do anything, back came the bee with dozens of brothers and friends and relations. They swarmed round James in glee, humming happily! Honey! Honey! How lovely! They settled on the little boy's hand and arm and front, and James beat them off.

'Go away! Go away!' he shouted. 'I don't want you!'

But the bees didn't understand. James ran away, right round the garden; but the bees flew after him in a crowd!

Then James smacked at them again, and one little bee stung him on the thumb and another stung him on the neck. How he yelled!

He rushed indoors to Mother, and the bees flew after him! James banged the door and ran into the hall, banging the hall door behind him too. Mother came running downstairs in alarm.

'I've been stung, I've been stung!' wept James. Mother looked at him – and she saw the honey on his arm and front.

'You can't complain about being stung,

31

James,' she said. 'You've been after the honey – and the bees are after it too! Why shouldn't they do what you do? I am not a bit sorry for you!'

She put some lotion on the stings, and washed the honey away. But she didn't say she was sorry, or comfort poor James. He did feel dreadful, and he was so ashamed of himself.

He has taken all the money out of his money-box now – one shilling and six pennies – and he is going to buy a new pot of honey for Mother. He thinks he will feel a bit better then – and I don't suppose he will steal any of *that*, do you?

THE STRANGE SPECTACLES

Once upon a time a little girl found a strange pair of spectacles. They were made of clear glass, but they had little silver specks in them that moved about like magic.

'Oh, I wonder if they *are* magic!' thought Freda. 'I'll put them on.'

So she popped them on her little nose – but to her disappointment everything looked exactly the same. So they couldn't be magic after all!

But they were, you know. As she looked round the field where she had found them, a small gnome put his head out of a door in a near-by tree.

'Freda!' he said. 'Those are my spectacles! Don't break them, will you?'

Freda jumped and turned round in fright. But the gnome had a kindly face and nodded at her. 'Don't be afraid,' he said. 'I don't mind you trying my spectacles on for a bit. They're magic you know!'

'Are they?' said Freda in surprise. 'I can't see that they are, little gnome. Everything looks just the same to me!'

'Ah, but when you look at *children*, you'll see something quite different!' said the gnome slyly.

'Those glasses will show you what children are really like! You borrow them and take them to school this afternoon. You'll see something strange!'

So Freda put the glasses carefully into her pocket and waited until she got to school that afternoon before she put them on. Then she slipped them on her nose and looked around to see if the glasses would show her what the children there were really like!

My goodness me! What a shock she got! The fat little girl next to her was nothing but a dressed-up little piggy-wig, with a fat face and snout, and tiny piggy eyes reading her book!

'Well, I always thought May was a greedy girl!' thought Freda. 'Yes – she's a little fat pig!'

She looked at spiteful little Annie who sat in front. Annie had a bad temper and she scratched people and pulled their hair. And do you know what Freda saw when she looked at Annie through her magic spectacles? She saw a small cat, with sharp claws for scratching and a spiteful little face!

Freda nearly laughed out loud. 'We often say that Annie is a spiteful little puss-cat!' she said to herself. 'And she is – all nicely dressed up in a red frock, and with a tail swinging angrily because she can't do her sums right!'

This was fun. Freda turned her eyes to Alex, a kindly boy, but so stupid that he could never say anything right. He just simply didn't use his brains. And he was a sheep! Yes, a nice, kindly, stupid-faced sheep, mumbling away to himself, trying to write out some words. Freda thought he looked too funny for anything!

Now what about Mollie, her best friend? She looked at her – and Mollie was a pretty little rabbit, with a woffly nose, big scared eyes, but kind and trustful and good. Freda smiled.

'That's just like Mollie!' she said in delight. 'A timid, shy little girl, but so kind and sweet. What about that peevish little Eric, though?'

Eric was a hedgehog, full of prickles! He bent over his work, his long prickles showing through his coat, and his snout almost touching the page.

'Of course!' said Freda. 'We often tell Eric he's as prickly as a hedgehog, always thinking we're teasing him when we're not!'

Freda thought this was lovely. What *would* all the children say if they knew what they looked like this afternoon? She looked at Joan, the head of the class, a clever, kind girl, always willing to look after anybody.

And Joan was a big, clever, kindly St Bernard dog, with bright kind eyes and such a lovely look of 'I'll take care of you all!' Freda was pleased. She had always liked Joan, and now she liked her even more.

Morris was another little pig, not quite so fat as May. John, a mean little boy whom nobody liked, was a cunning-looking rat. Freda didn't like the look of him at all. She turned her head away quickly. How horrid he looked!

Dear old stupid Winnie, another one who wouldn't use her brains, was – what do you think? A grey donkey! Freda almost laughed out loud when she saw Winnie's long grey nose bent over her book and the big ears sticking straight up.

Elsie was another rabbit. Perky little Lucy, black-eyed, friendly, and merry, was a robin! Her sharp beak followed her lines of writing, and she blinked her black eyes as she wrote. A robin! Of course! Lucy had always reminded Freda of a perky robin.

Big Janet had always made her think of a fussy old hen, fussing and worrying and scratching round – and dear me, there she sat fluffing up her feathers found the collar of her jersey, looking anxiously round to see that everyone was all right! And what do you suppose dear old Susie was – a goose, yes, a nice fluffy goose!

Freda looked at Harry, a snappy little boy with a bad temper. He was a little snapping dog, showing his teeth at Elsie the rabbit! She had borrowed his rubber and he was being snappy about it. 'Yes,' thought Freda. 'He really is just like a snappy little dog-in-the-manger!'

Then Miss Brown the teacher spoke sharply. 'Freda! Do your work! Don't look round the room and dream!'

Freda went red. She took off the magic spectacles and went on with her work. When next she looked up all the children had gone back to their right shape – but ah, Freda knew what they were *really* like, didn't she!

She took the strange spectacles back to the gnome the next day. 'They are wonderful!' she said. 'But there's just one thing I wish – and that is that I could see *myself* through them! I'd like to know what *I* am really like too!'

'Well, you should have looked at yourself in the glass!' said the gnome with a smile, and he slipped inside his house in the tree and shut the door.

So Freda doesn't know what she is really like, any more than you do. I wonder what she would have seen if she had looked at *you*? Think a minute and see if you know!

THE TWO BAD BOYS

There were once two bad boys called Tom and Jim. They were not truthful and they were not honest – in fact, they stole apples from outside shops, and once Tom had taken a full milk-bottle from a doorstep!

This was really dreadful. The apples were green and gave them both a pain, and Tom fell with the milk-bottle, broke it, and cut his hand, so they didn't get any good out of their stealing; but how sad their mothers were to know they had children like that!

'Nobody gets happiness out of badness,' said Tom's mother, as she bandaged his hand.

Tom didn't believe her – but when he found that the Sunday-school party was going to be held on Saturday and that he and Jim were not invited, he began to wish he hadn't been so bad!

He grumbled about it to Jim. 'There's going to be crackers and balloons and blow-up pigs that squeak, and all kinds of goodies and oranges and sweets and a toy for everybody!' he said. 'I wish we were going.'

'Well!' said Jim. 'What about creeping in before the party begins and taking a few things for ourselves? We could easily do that. We could creep in at a window.'

Jim was a very bad boy as you can see. Tom nodded his head. 'All right,' he said. 'We will. Let's go and peep in at the window on Friday and see what sort of toys are there.'

So on Friday they peeped in at the window. They saw Mrs Jones and Miss Brown arranging everything ready for the next day. They saw the dishes of sweets put out, the plates of oranges. There were no cakes or buns yet, because they would be made next day. They saw the big balloons being blown up, and watched the balloon-pigs being stood all down the table for the children.

There was a big table for the toys too. My goodness, what lovely toys! There were two big humming-tops, a train that could whistle, a doll that could say 'Ma-ma, Pa-pa!', some tiny motor-cars with little hooters, a bear that growled, a mouse that squeaked – oh, more toys than Tom and Jim could count.

They watched until Mrs Jones and Miss Brown put the light out and went away. Then the boys spoke to one another.

'We'll come tomorrow, when the windows will be opened to air the room – and we'll take oranges, sweets, balloons, crackers, and toys!'

They slipped away, thinking nobody had heard them. But the toys had both seen *and* heard them! They knew Tom and Jim all right!

Everybody knew about the two bad boys!

'Did you hear what they said?' cried the bear, in excitement. 'We won't let them steal us! We'll give them such a fright!'

So when the next night came, and the two naughty boys crept in at an open window, the toys were ready. The mouse had taken three of the balloon-pigs from the table, and he and the doll and the bear pulled the little corks from the pigs' mouths as soon as the boys came in.

You know what a noise a balloon-pig makes when the air goes out of him, don't you? 'Eeeeeeeeeeeeeee!' they all said in mournful voices. 'Eeeeeeeeeeeeeeee!'

Tom and Jim stood still in fright. Whatever was that? The pigs stopped making a noise and fell over, quite flat. Then the teddy-bear pressed himself in the middle.

'Grrrrrrrr!' he said. 'Grrrrrrrrrrr!'

'Oooooooh!' said Tom and Jim. 'Is it a dog growling?'

'Grrrrrrrr!' said the bear again, quite enjoying himself. Then the mouse and the other toys took the three humming-tops and set them spinning madly on the floor. They all hummed like enormous bees!

'Zoooooooooom! Zooooooooom! Zeeeeeeeeem! Zoooooooooom!' they went. Tom tried to run away and he fell over a mat that caught his foot. Bang!

'Ow!' cried Tom. 'Something's caught me!

What's making that noise? Are we in a bee-hive? I wish we could see, but the room's all dark!'

The mouse pressed himself in the middle and made loud squeaks. 'Eeoo, eeoo, eeoo, eeoo!' Jim fell over Tom in fright. The mouse nearly laughed out loud!

Then the engine of the train began to whistle. 'Pheeeeeeee!' it went, as loudly as it could. Good gracious, what a fright it gave the two bad boys! They could hardly get up!

'Where's the window? Where's the window?' cried Jim.

Now the talking doll began to call 'Mama, Papa, Mama, Papa! at the top of her voice, and the golly and bear pressed the little hooters of the motor cars at the same time.

'Honk, honk, honk! Honk, Mama, Papa, honk, honk, Mama, honk, Papa, honk!' What a noise! Tom and Jim rushed for the window and tried to climb through – and then the mouse had a bright idea. He took, the brooch off his coat and drove the pin into a big balloon hanging near him.

'BANG!' It went off with such a loud pop that even the toys were startled. Jim and Tom fell to the ground.

'I'm shot!' groaned Tom.

'So am I!' cried Jim. 'Somebody's shot us. Didn't you hear the bang?'

And there they lay groaning, thinking that they were shot, till the door opened and in trooped all the children that had been invited to the party. How surprised they were to see Tom and Jim – and you may be sure they guessed at once what those two bad boys had come for!

They shooed them out of the door, they laughed at them – and they banged the door behind them. Tom and Jim began to cry. How they wished they could go and join the happy children in the gay room, with all the balloons and toys!

'It's our own fault,' said Tom, wiping his eyes. 'Mother says nobody gets any happiness out of being bad. I'm going to be good for a change. I've had a real fright tonight, and I'm going home to find out where I've been shot!'

Well, he won't find where he's shot, and neither will Jim – but the toys will have done a good deed if they have stopped those two boys from being bad. The mouse still laughs when he remembers all that happened that evening.

THE THREE LOVELY PRESENTS

Daddy was going away for a whole week and the three children were sad. They hated their Daddy to go away.

'Mummy will miss you,' said Janet.

'So will we,' said Dan.

'We'll love to see you back on Saturday,' said Rosy, and they all gave Daddy a hug.

'What will you bring?' asked Dan.

'I shall bring back with me a new wheelbarrow – a fine digging-spade – and a green watering-can!' said Daddy.

'Good!' said Dan, who longed for a spade to dig up his garden.

'Lovely!' said Janet, who had always wanted a wheelbarrow.

'Ooooh!' said Rosy, who simply loved watering her flowers. They were all good gardeners and had little gardens of their own.

'Good-bye!' said Daddy. 'Be good, and help Mummy all you can!' Then he jumped into his car, started it, and off he went down the road.

Mummy was going to be very busy whilst Daddy was away. She was going to do some spring-cleaning!

'You can really help me a lot,' she said to the

children, 'and Daddy will be so pleased to see everything shining and bright when he gets home.'

But, dear me, when Mummy found something she wanted Dan to do, he sulked and wouldn't do it! It was when Mummy found that she had come to the end of her soap, and she asked Dan to run down to the grocer's and get her some more.

'I'm busy reading,' sulked Dan. 'You always ask me to do errands when I'm reading, Mummy.'

'Will *you* go for me, Janet?' said Mummy, looking rather sad.

But Janet was busy too. She was washing her dolls' frocks. 'Can't I go when I've finished this?' she said.

Rosy was busy tidying the toy cupboard. She looked up. 'Mummy, I'll go!' she said. 'It won't take me a minute.' And it didn't. She popped on her hat, ran down the road, and was back in a trice with the soap. Mummy was very pleased.

The next day Mummy wanted some daffodils picked out of the garden and put into a vase for the table, because Aunt Ellen was coming to tea and she wanted her table to look nice.

'Janet dear, run and pick some daffies for me!' said Mummy.

'Oh, bother!' said Janet.

'Well, perhaps Dan will go,' said Mummy.

But Dan was far too busy. Rosy jumped up and said never mind, *she* would go. So down the garden she went and picked a fine bunch of daffodils. She arranged them beautifully in a vase, and put them on the table. As she did so she trod on Janet's toe, quite by accident.

'Oh, you clumsy girl!' cried Janet. 'Look where you're going! I shan't lend you my new wheelbarrow if you're not careful!'

'Sorry,' said Rosy. 'You shouldn't stick your feet out so far.'

That night everybody forgot to put Sandy the dog into his kennel, and Mummy suddenly remembered just as it was bedtime for the children.

'Oh, dear!' she said. 'We've forgotten Sandy! Who will take the torch and put him into his kennel for me?'

Dan said nothing; he didn't like the dark. Janet thought it was raining and she didn't want to go out. So Rosy thought she had better find the torch and take Sandy, or else Mummy would have to do it.

'You're very selfish,' she said to Dan as she went to find the torch. 'You just don't do anything.'

'If you talk to me like that, you shan't use my new spade when Daddy brings it,' said Dan sharply.

'I don't care,' said Rosy. 'I shall have my new watering-can!' She found the torch and ran

'I'm afraid Rosy must have all the garden things'

out in the dark with Sandy. It wasn't raining, and there was a lovely moon, so she didn't need the torch after all. Sandy went into his kennel and curled up on the straw.

The next day Pussy was very naughty. She jumped up on the table, when nobody was in the room, and began to drink the milk out of the jug there. When Janet came into the room Pussy was frightened and jumped down. But her claws caught in the tablecloth and down it came, and all the tea-things with it. The milk spilt all over the floor, and the jam-pot broke. Oh, what a mess of plates and milk and jam!

'Mummy! Mummy!' shouted Janet. 'Pussy has knocked over all the tea-things!'

'Oh, Janet!' cried Mummy. 'What a nuisance! Do clear up the mess, like a good girl, because I'm in the middle of putting up new curtains in your room, and I just want to finish them.'

Janet looked at the mess and sulked. Why should she have to clear up what Pussy had spilt? She was just going out to play, and it would take a long time to clear up everything. Then she saw Dan coming in, and she called to him.

'Dan! Look what Pussy's done! I'm just going out and Mummy wants all this cleared up. Will you do it?' And before Dan could say yes or no, the naughty little girl had run out to play next door. Dan stared at the mess and frowned.

'I'm jolly well not going to clear this up,' he thought. 'Why should I? Mummy will easily clear it up when she comes down.'

So Dan slipped out too, and went to play with George, who had a fine railway set, over the road.

Soon Rosy came in – and when she saw the dreadful mess all over the dining-room, she did get a shock.

'Oh dear!' she said. 'I suppose Pussy has done this! I'd better clear up the things in case Mummy comes down and gets upset.'

So Rosy picked up all the tea-things, wiped up the spilt milk and the jam, and tried to mend the jam-pot with glue. Then she washed up the dirty things and cleared everything away neatly.

Mummy didn't come downstairs until all the children were back again, and were sitting at the table doing their home-work. She was so pleased when the saw the upset tea-things cleared away.

'Thank you, Janet,' she said gratefully. 'It was good of you to clear up the mess of spilt milk and jam and put everything away.'

Janet went red. 'I didn't clear it up,' she said, surprised. 'I told Dan to. I was just going out.'

Then it was Dan's turn to go red. For Mummy turned to him and said, 'Thank you, Dan dear. That was very kind of you.'

'I didn't do it,' said Dan, but he wished he had.

'I did it, Mummy,' said Rosy, looking up from her spelling. 'It didn't take me a minute.'

'You're a real help to me, Rosy,' said Mummy, and she kissed her. Janet and Dan were still red. They wished that Mummy had kissed them too.

Well, the next excitement was Daddy coming home again! The three children were all at the window watching for the car, and at last it drew up at the gate. Janet gave a shriek of delight.

'Look at the parcels in the back! I can see my wheelbarrow with its one wheel sticking out. And it's got a rubber tyre on!'

'And I can see the handle of my spade!' shouted Dan, running to the door.

'And I can see the spout of my watering-can!' said Rosy; and out they all ran to welcome Daddy. He came in with all the presents and his bag. He hugged everybody and asked Mummy how she was.

'Splendid,' said Mummy. 'And all the spring-clearing is done. So I have had a very good week.'

'And have the children helped you?' asked Daddy.

Mummy looked rather solemn. 'Well,' she said, I've had a lot of things done for me. I ran out of soap and somebody ran down to the grocer's and fetched it for me.'

'Good,' said Daddy. 'Who was that?'

'Rosy!' said Mummy, and Daddy gave her a hug.

'Then I wanted some daffies picked and put into a vase when Aunt Ellen came to tea,' said Mummy, 'and somebody did them most beautifully for me, without a single grumble.'

'Fine!' said Daddy, looking at Dan and Janet and wondering which of them it was. 'Who was that?'

'Rosy!' said Mummy, and Rosy got another hug. Then Mummy went on: 'And one night we forgot about putting Sandy into his kennel, so somebody got the torch and went out to put him in for me.'

'Splendid!' said Daddy. 'I wonder who that was?'

'Rosy!' said Mummy, and Rosy got a kiss. 'And another time Pussy jumped out on the table and upset all the things on the floor,' said Mummy. 'Somebody cleared them all up without being asked – though the somebody who *was* asked didn't do it!'

'And who was the somebody who did it without being asked?' said Daddy. 'Was it Rosy *again*?'

'It was,' said Mummy, and Rosy got such a hug that she lost her breath. 'Daddy, Rosy has been the greatest help, but I'm afraid the others haven't really tried. Isn't it a pity?'

'A great pity,' said Daddy, undoing the three lovely presents he had brought. 'I'm afraid Rosy must have *all* the garden things! Rosy, here is the spade – and the wheelbarrow – and the watering-can – with my love and best thanks for being good to Mummy for me whilst I was away.'

Janet and Dan burst into tears. 'But, Daddy, you promised you would bring us those!' wept Janet.

'Yes, I promised to bring the presents,' said Daddy, 'but I didn't say who was going to have them! And as you have done nothing to deserve them, Rosy must have them all!'

So Rosy did; but you know she really is a most unselfish little girl, for she lets Dan use the lovely big spade, and she lets Janet have the wheelbarrow whenever she asks for it. Don't you think it's nice of her?

Do you think you would have won one of those lovely presents? I am sure you would!

HE WOULDN'T WIPE HIS SHOES

Kenneth was always getting into trouble because he wouldn't wipe his shoes! He used to go out into the garden to play, and then come straight in without wiping his feet even once on the mat.

So he left muddy marks on the carpet, and you could always see where he had walked in the house because there was mud everywhere! He really was naughty.

'Wipe your feet, Kenneth!' his mother said each time he came in.

'Wipe your feet, Kenneth,' his aunt said when he went to see her on Saturdays.

'Wipe your feet, Kenneth,' his teacher said to him each day at school. But did he wipe his feet? No, not if he could possibly slip indoors without doing so! And even when he *did* wipe them, it was what his mother called a lick and a promise!

Now one day Kenneth and the other children in his class were told that there was to be a match between the five classes to see who could win the most marks for good manners. The teachers wanted to find out which was the best-mannered class, and all the children were told they could win marks for their own class by trying hard.

'What sort of manners will count for marks?' asked Harold.

'Well,' said the teacher, 'all good manners will count, Harold. Boys raise their caps to ladies – that is good manners. Children give up their seats to grown-ups in buses and trams – that is good manners. Saying please and thank you – standing back for others to pass – opening doors for grown-ups – never pushing – wiping your shoes – shutting doors quietly behind you – all these things are good manners, and you can win marks for them this week.'

'Suppose we *don't* do something we should?' asked Harold.

'Well, I'm afraid bad manners will make you *lose* a mark!' said the teacher. Harold gazed round at Kenneth.

'Ha!' he said, 'I guess you'll make us lose all the marks we earn, Kenneth, by forgetting to wipe your feet every time you come in! Bother you!'

Kenneth went red. 'I'll try,' he said.

He did try – but you know he had forgotten for so long that he really couldn't remember even when he tried! So he lost a great many marks each day for the class, and they were very angry.

'It's too bad of you,' said Harold to Kenneth at the end of the week. 'Our class is bottom for good manners! And it's all because you kept losing us marks for not wiping your feet. Horrid boy!'

Kenneth was unhappy. How dreadful to try hard over something and still not be able to remember! He ran home, wondering how he could cure himself.

That afternoon Mother sent him to the cobbler's with a pair of shoes to be mended. The cobbler was a little man, bent double over his shoe-making, and he was so old that he had even forgotten himself how old he was. Kenneth thought he must be about a hundred.

'Good afternoon, little man,' he said to Kenneth, peering at him from behind thick glasses. 'And how's the world using you?'

'Not very well,' said Kenneth, and he told the cobbler how he had made his class bottom for the week, all because he simply could *not* remember to wipe his feet when he came in.

'Very bad, very bad,' said the old cobbler. 'Don't you know that damp mud is bad for shoes? Ah, you should take care of shoes, my boy. If you had made as many as I had, of good stout leather, you would be very careful of them, yes, you would. Now, I remember when I was a lad, my brother was the same as you – never wiped his shoes once. Ah, but he was cured!'

'Was he?' asked Kenneth. 'How was he cured? Could I be cured too?'

'Yes, for sure!' said the old man, and he

54

chuckled like a hen clucking. 'Now see, young man – take this tin home, and clean your shoes with this bit of yellow polish I put inside. Clean all your outdoor shoes with it, and I tell you, you'll soon be cured, just as my brother was. Ho, ho, ho! He was cured all right!'

But he wouldn't tell Kenneth how, and the boy ran home with the tin of yellow polish, wondering whatever cure it could be. He didn't really like to try it – but at last, thinking that it couldn't possibly hurt him, he took all his outdoor shoes and boots, found a shoebrush, and set to work to polish his shoes with the yellow polish.

His shoes shone brilliantly. It was marvellous polish. Kenneth slipped on his outdoor boots and went to afternoon school. Of course, he quite forgot to wipe his feet as usual. In he went, stepping on the mat, but not rubbing his feet at all.

He was a bit late. He took his place, and found his book – and then he noticed that his feet felt dreadfully uncomfortable. His boots seemed to be growing smaller and smaller, tighter and tighter. At last poor Kenneth couldn't bear them on his feet! He undid the laces and took off his muddy boots, hoping that the master would not see him.

And what do you think happened? Why, as soon as his boots were off, they ran over to the mat by themselves, making a tremendous clatter! When they got to the mat, they wiped themselves thoroughly, scraping all the mud off as carefully as could be!

Everyone looked up when they heard the clatter – and how they stared when they saw Kenneth's big boots running over to the mat, dragging their laces behind them. Then they began to laugh. *How* they laughed! Even the master laughed till the tears ran down his cheeks!

'Ho, ho, ho! Ha, ha, ha! Look at those boots! Kenneth can't remember to wipe his own boots, so they're doing it for themselves! For shame, Kenneth! Ho, ho, ho!'

Kenneth went very red. He hated being laughed at. He sat looking very ashamed until his boots, now perfectly clean, came clattering back to him. He put them on. They seemed quite the right size now.

Everyone was talking about the wonderful boots that Friday afternoon, but Kenneth didn't want to join in. He ran home, and burst in at the door, longing to take off those dreadful boots! But as soon as he got in, he saw his Uncle George there.

'Hallo, hallo!' said Uncle George. 'Here comes the thunderstorm!'

Kenneth ran to hug his uncle, for he was very fond of him. He quite forgot to wipe his feet, of course – but it wasn't very long before his boots reminded him!

They suddenly grew so tight that Kenneth

As soon as his boots were off, they ran over to the mat by themselves

almost squealed out. He undid the laces hurriedly – and, oh dear, those boots ran out of the room, all the way down the hall to the front-door mat, where they could be heard busily wiping the mud off the soles and heels!

'Goodness gracious me!' said Uncle George, in the greatest astonishment.

'Well, I never!' said Mother. And they both began to laugh till they cried! Kenneth didn't laugh. He felt very angry with himself.

Well, so things went on all the week-end. It didn't matter which pair of outdoor boots or shoes Kenneth put on, they had all been polished with the yellow polish, and they each ran off to the mat to wipe themselves if Kenneth forgot – which he usually did!

By the time he got back to school on Monday the word had gone round that there was something very exciting about Kenneth's shoes, and all the boys and girls were longing to watch Kenneth forget to wipe his feet.

But for once in a way Kenneth didn't forget! No – he really remembered, and he stood on the mat, wiping his feet just as all the others did. But poor Kenneth – he had left just a little bit of mud at the back of his left foot, and the boot knew it all right. It grew tighter and tighter till Kenneth had to take it off – then away to the mat it ran, and wiped itself well till the tiny bit of mud had gone.

'This is dreadful!' thought Kenneth. 'Not

only have I got to remember to wipe my feet — but I've got to wipe every speck of mud off too. I shall never, never do it, and all my life I shall be laughed at because my boots and shoes run to the mat to wipe themselves. Oh, how I wish I had never told that old cobbler about myself!'

Well, the yellow polish lasted until Kenneth's feet grew too big for his boots. Then he had to have new ones, and he begged the cobbler not to rub any of his strange polish on them.

'Ah, but are you sure you're cured?' said the old man, with his clucking chuckle.

'Quite sure,' said Kenneth firmly. 'I haven't forgotten to wipe my feet for ages, and I'm sure I never shall again. So please let me have my new boots and shoes without any yellow polish at all.'

'Very well,' said the cobbler, and he kept his word. Kenneth's new boots and shoes were the same as yours and mine, and so far Kenneth has not forgotten once to wipe his feet on the mat.

His mother has still got his old boots and shoes, and she says she is waiting to give them to any boy or girl who has a bad memory for wiping feet! So let me know if your mother thinks you need them, and if they are your size you had better have them!

SILLY COUSIN ANN!

'Cousin Ann is coming to stay with you for a week,' said Mother one day. 'You can go to the station and meet her this afternoon. You must give her a nice time. She is as old as Mary, so you should have some fun together.'

Dick, Mary and John were pleased. It would be nice to have someone else to play with.

'I'll show her my caterpillars,' said John.

'I'll show her the best tree in the garden to climb,' said Dick.

'And I'll show her Mr Brown's old cart-horse who leans over the gate and lets us stroke her soft nose,' said Mary.

Ann was a little girl, not as big as Mary, though she was the same age. She seemed very quiet, but the other children thought perhaps she was shy. On the way home from the station they passed the field gate where Blossom, the old brown cart-horse, lived. Mary whistled loudly, and put her hand into her pocket for the lump of sugar she had brought for Blossom.

'Look, Ann, here comes Blossom,' said Mary, as the great old horse came lumbering up. She put her enormous head right over the gate and nearly touched Ann's shoulder. She shrieked and ran to the other side of the road.

'Ann! Blossom won't hurt you!' cried Mary. 'Come here and stroke her nose.'

'No, no!' said Ann, quite pale with fright. 'She might bite me.'

'She won't, really she won't,' said Mary patiently. 'Come and give her this lump of sugar, Ann.'

But Ann wouldn't. Nothing would make her go near the old horse, so the children went home thinking that Ann was really rather silly.

'Come and see what I've got, Ann,' said John, who was longing to show his cousin his fine caterpillars. They were stick-caterpillars, and when they were still they looked exactly like bits of twig or stick. John thought they were wonderful. Ann went with him, thinking she was going to see some soldiers, or perhaps a fine train. John took her to the shed, and there he showed her a box full of big caterpillars, all eating busily.

'Oh, the horrid things!' squealed Ann, drawing back quickly when she saw them. 'I can't bear caterpillars! Oh, John, how can you touch them? Oh, I couldn't! I don't like caterpillars, or earwigs, or spiders, or moths, or beetles, or . . .'

'Well, I think you are perfectly silly then,' said John impatiently. 'What harm can they do you? None at all! They are far more frightened of *you* than you of them. Fancy being frightened of such tiny things! You ought to be ashamed of yourself.'

Ann began to cry. She did not like being spoken to like that.

'I think you are horrid,' she said. 'I do really. I wish I hadn't come now. I want to go home.'

Dick felt very sorry for the little girl. He took her hand. 'Never mind,' he said; 'forget about caterpillars, and spiders and things. Come with me and I'll show you something fine!'

He took her to a big chestnut tree at the bottom of the garden. 'Do you see that branch up there?' he said. 'Well, that's our secret home. The trunk is hollow just there and we keep a box of biscuits there, and a cushion to sit on, and some stories to read! I'll take you up, if you like. Come on!'

Dick swung himself up on to a branch and stood on it, ready to climb upwards. But Ann went quite white and shook her head.

'Oh, I couldn't climb a tree,' she said. 'I'd be so afraid of falling! Oh, I really couldn't, Dick. Please, please come down. I can't bear to see you up there in case you fall.'

'You *are* a little coward!' said Dick scornfully. 'Go and play by yourself! I'm going up to our secret place!' And up he went, whilst poor Ann stood below, looking up in fright, afraid that Dick would fall at any moment. But he didn't. He took out the cushion, put it on a branch, and sat on it. He took a biscuit from the tin and

'You are a little coward. Go and play by yourself!'

pulled out a paper to read. 'Go away!' he said to Ann. 'I don't want you.'

Ann wandered away. She wished she had never come. 'I can't help being frightened of things,' she said with tears in her eyes. 'I'm not really a coward. It's just that I'm frightened of some things.'

Ann didn't have a very nice time the next few days. Dick put an earwig on her plate and made her upset her lemonade in fright. Mary put a spider on her pillow, and Ann refused to get into bed. She made such a noise that Mother came to see what was the matter. She took the spider gently off the pillow and put it outside. Then she tucked Ann up and kissed her. She went into Mary's room, and called Dick and John in too.

'You are not being kind,' she said. 'Don't you think that Ann is frightened of quite enough things, poor child, without you frightening her still more? I don't think she is a coward, really. She just can't *help* being afraid of some things. Even grown-ups are like that sometimes. I know someone who is terrified of bats!'

'How silly of them!' said John. 'They are only little flying mice!'

'It isn't good manners to tease a visitor, and it certainly isn't kind,' said Mother. 'I shall expect you to behave differently for the rest of Ann's visit.'

So after that the children didn't frighten Ann

any more, but they let her play alone and didn't speak to her more than they could help.

Mother told them to go for a picnic on the last day of Ann's stay, so they set off to the woods with a big basket. Ann was very miserable. She knew her cousins thought her a silly little coward and were longing for her to go home.

After tea the two boys and Mary went to hunt for a good tree to climb. And it was whilst John was up in the top branches that he caught sight of something struggling in the river not far off. He told the others to go and see what it was. They ran off.

They soon found out. A puppy had fallen into the river and had got caught in some weeds. He could not get out and he was struggling hard. The old lady who owned him was on the bank, looking up and down for someone to help her.

'Oh, dear!' she said when she saw the children. 'My little puppy is drowning. Is there any grown-up with you who can help me?'

'No,' said Dick. 'Oh, poor little thing! What can we do?'

'I can do something,' said Ann suddenly. She slipped off her shoes and threw her hat on the ground. She jumped straight into the river with a splash, and to everyone's great surprise swam strongly over to the weeds in the middle of the river.

'Ann! Ann! Be careful!' shouted Dick, afraid his cousin would drown. 'Oh, dear! If only Mother was here!'

John climbed down his tree and raced to the others. 'What did you tell Ann to do that for?' he said.

'We didn't,' said Mary. 'She did it herself. Oh, look! – she has reached the puppy. She is pulling him out of the weeds! – he's free! Now he's swimming towards the bank! Oh, good!'

Sure enough the puppy was swimming towards them. Ann turned round in the water and swam back too. She was a splendid swimmer. Her cousins had not known that she could swim at all. In fact, they had thought her such a silly that they didn't think she could do such a thing as swim! Ann swam to the bank and climbed up. She was dripping wet, but her eyes were happy.

'I'm so glad I got him for you,' she said to the old lady. 'I love dogs.'

'You are the bravest little girl I've ever seen!' said the old lady. 'These other children only stood and stared, but you jumped in.'

'But you see, I'm a very strong swimmer,' said Ann quickly. 'It would be silly to jump in if you couldn't swim well. Mary and Dick and John do things I'm afraid of doing, and perhaps I can do things they can't do too.'

'You can, Ann!' said Dick, putting his arm round his wet cousin and giving her a hug. 'I'm proud you are my cousin. I shouldn't have dared to jump in, because I can only swim a little way – and Mary and John can't swim at all! I'm sorry we said you were a silly little coward. You're not! You are just as brave as we are at some things!'

Ann was very happy that her cousins were being so nice to her. They took her home and told Mother how brave she had been. Mother was pleased. She took Ann's wet clothes and put them to dry.

'Mother, we haven't been very nice to Ann this week,' said John, rather ashamed of himself. 'Could you ask her to stay another week – then we could be really nice and make up for this horrid week?'

'I don't expect Ann will want to stay,' said Mother. 'She hasn't been happy, I know.'

But Ann did want to stay!

'Yes, I'd love to!' she said. 'Now that the others know I'm not really a silly, I'd like to stay another week. I would like to learn not to be afraid of horses and spiders and climbing trees, and perhaps I could teach my cousins to swim, so that they wouldn't be afraid of jumping into the water.'

So Ann stayed another week; and at the end of the time Dick could swim right across the river, and John and Mary could swim twelve strokes each and were not a bit afraid of the water. And as for Ann, she learnt to climb an easy tree, and to give Blossom a piece of sugar, and not to run away from a spider. So I think they all did very well indeed!

BAD-TEMPERED BETTY

Betty was such an impatient little girl! She always wanted everything at once, and if people didn't do things quickly enough for her she lost her temper and stamped and screamed.

It was dreadful – and nobody knew what to do with her. If she played with somebody else it always ended in screams and sobs. Even when gentle John came to play, it was the same.

'Let's play engines,' said John.

'I want to be the engine-driver,' said Betty. 'You stand here and I'll drive you. When I punch you like that you must go fast – and when I pinch you like that, you must go slow.'

John didn't like that at all, but he tried to please Betty. He didn't go fast enough for her, and she shouted at him. He didn't stop soon enough, and she pinched him so hard that he almost cried.

'I don't like this game,' he said. 'Let's play another, where you're one side of the garden and I'm the other side.'

Betty stamped her foot. 'No, we're going to play engines,' she said. 'If we don't, I'll scream, and then Mother will come out, and I'll tell her you've been smacking me.'

Well, that was the way Betty behaved, and if you know anyone like that you'll guess how dreadful it was to go to tea with her, or to play in the garden for the morning.

One day Mother had a letter from an old friend of hers. 'Listen, Betty,' she said. 'Auntie Ellen has asked you to go and stay for a few days with her. Would you like to go? There is a lovely garden there, with lots of fruit, and she has a little boy a year younger than you. It would be fun for you, wouldn't it?'

Betty loved fruit, and she thought it would be nice to go. So that day her mother packed a little bag of clothes for her, and took Betty by train to Aunt Ellen's.

'What a lovely house!' thought Betty, when she saw it. 'And oh, what a lovely garden! Look at the gooseberries – and the peas – and the cherries – and the currants! Oh, I'm going to have a good time here!'

'Peter is out at present with his nurse,' said Auntie Ellen, a fat, nice-smelling lady. 'When he comes in, you and he will be able to have a nice game together in the nursery. You will be kind to him, won't you, because he is not quite as big as you.'

'Yes, Betty, do try and be kind and good,' said Betty's mother as she kissed her goodbye. 'Don't be impatient, dear, and don't lose your temper.'

It wasn't long before Peter came in with his

nurse. Betty went upstairs with him. He was not so big as she was, and he was very spoilt indeed – so spoilt that he was every bit as bad as Betty! He knew all about stamping and sulking and screaming, and pinching and kicking, I can tell you! My goodness, he was a dreadful child!

At first he was quite polite. 'What shall we play at?' he asked.

'Let's have all your toys out and look at them,' said Betty.

'Change your shoes first, Peter,' said the nurse, and she went out of the room. Peter threw off his walking shoes and took up his indoor shoes. They had buttons. He did one shoe up but he couldn't do the other.

'Do it up for me, Betty,' he said. So Betty bent to do it up. But it was a stiff button and took her a long time.

'Oh, hurry up, hurry up!' shouted Peter suddenly. 'What a slow-coach you are!'

'How impatient you are!' said Betty. 'How can I do it up if you wriggle like that?'

'You're just a silly slow-coach of a girl!' said Peter, and he kicked out at her with his shoe. So after that Betty wouldn't do it up. She walked to the toy cupboard and opened it. Inside there were more toys than she could count.

She took out a box of soldiers – but Peter grabbed them from her.

'You shan't play with those!' he said. 'Soldiers

are for boys, not for girls.'

'Well, you've got dolls here, and they are for girls, not for boys!' said Betty. 'Ha, ha!'

'Don't "ha-ha" at me like that!' said Peter, and he slammed the toy cupboard door so hard that it trapped Betty's finger and she began to cry.

'Cry-baby, cry-baby!' said Peter.

Betty glared at him and stopped. She found a box of bricks and began to build a tower with them.

'I want to play too,' said Peter. 'Look, let's build it like *this*!'

'No, my way's best,' said Betty. 'Let me do it my way.'

Peter stamped in a rage. He wasn't used to someone like Betty. Most children were afraid of him, but Betty was such a bad-tempered child herself that she wanted her own way too!

'I tell you, they're my bricks, and I shall say how they're to be played with!' he shouted. 'I'll knock your tower down.'

'No, you won't,' said Betty, and she stood in front of him. Peter flew at her and she fell over, knocking her own tower down. She screamed – and the nurse came in.

'Whatever is the matter?' she said.

'Betty knocked her own tower down and she is crying because of that,' said Peter. 'It wouldn't have fallen down if she had built it the way *I* wanted to.'

'Oh, you naughty story-teller, you horrid

little boy!' sobbed Betty.

'Now, now, you mustn't talk like that,' said the nurse. 'That is naughty. Put the bricks away and wash your hands. It is tea-time.'

The two children went to the bathroom. Betty turned on the taps and took up the soap.

'Oh, do hurry up,' said Peter impatiently. 'You are the slowest person I ever knew.'

Betty still felt very angry, but she was rather afraid of the nurse, so she said nothing. She could see that Peter's nurse thought the world of him, and she was afraid that she would always stick up for Peter, whether he was right or wrong.

There was a plate of chocolate biscuits at tea-time, and both children loved these. When there was only one left, they both snatched for it.

'*I* ought to have it, I'm the visitor!' shouted Betty.

'*I* ought to have it because I'm younger than you are!' shouted back Peter.

'You're a greedy, bad-mannered boy,' said Betty, losing her temper.

'Now, now, Betty, what is this I hear?' said Aunt Ellen, suddenly opening the door and coming into the room. 'Are you calling my dear little Peterkin rude names? He is younger and smaller than you. For shame! Your mother told me you were rather bad-tempered, but I did think you would behave properly when you were a visitor!'

She fell over, knocking her own tower down

'Peter's much more bad-tempered!' said Betty, almost crying. 'I don't like him.'

'Well, I don't like you either!' said Peter. 'People don't like bad-tempered children, do they, Mother?'

'Of course not,' said Aunt Ellen, staring at Betty sternly.

Betty didn't say anything more. She drank her tea and glared at Peter. She did wish she hadn't come to stay with him.

The next day was even worse. Betty was in the garden, and she wanted to pick some gooseberries to eat. But Peter wouldn't let her.

'They're *our* gooseberries, not yours,' he said, 'and I won't let you have any because you are rude and bad-tempered.'

'Well, so are you!' shouted Betty, in a rage. 'So you shan't have any either.'

'I shall then!' said Peter, 'because they are mine!' And he picked a handful of the ripest red gooseberries and ate them, and then shook some cherries down from a cherry tree. But not one would he give Betty.

'You be good-tempered and play the game I want to play and I'll give you some cherries,' said Peter at last.

'Well, what game shall we play?' asked Betty sulkily.

'We'll play engines,' said Peter. 'You be the engine and I'll be the engine-driver.'

'No,' said Betty. 'I'll be the driver!'

Peter stamped his foot in rage. '*I* want to be the driver, *I* want to . . .' he began.

'All right, all right,' said Betty. 'Go on. Drive me, then.'

'When I punch you like this, you must go fast,' said Peter, giving Betty a punch in the back, 'and when I pinch you like this, you must stop.'

Betty remembered something very suddenly, and she went red. Hadn't she said just those same things to John – and to many others too, when they had come to play with her? How horrid she must have seemed to them! – just as horrid as Peter seemed to her.

'Oh, go on, go on, slow-coach!' yelled Peter, giving her a hard punch. 'You don't go fast enough. Now we're coming to a station, where that tree is. Stop! Stop, I say!'

He pinched Betty hard and she felt the tears coming into her eyes.

'I don't like this game,' she said. 'Let's play another, where you're at the top of the garden and I'm at the bottom.'

Peter stamped and screamed. 'Play this game, play this!' he shouted. 'I'll scream again and make Nurse come out.'

Betty lost her temper with the naughty boy and shouted back at him, 'Scream then – I'll tell your nurse how you behave!'

So Peter screamed, and when his nurse came out he sobbed and told her that Betty had been smacking him – and the worst of it was that the nurse believed him.

'I have heard that you are an unkind, bad-tempered little girl,' she said to Betty. 'Other nurses have told me so. How can you behave like that! Come, Peter darling, you shall pick cherries with me, and Betty, you can stay indoors.'

Well, it went on like that all the time, and at last Betty found that it was easier to be nice to Peter, although he was so horrid, than to be nasty, because if she was as bad to him as he was to her, he told tales on her, and Betty got punished!

How glad she was when her stay came to an end and she went home!

'Did you have a nice time, darling?' asked her mother.

'No, Mummy,' said Betty, and she told her mother all about how bad-tempered, impatient, and unkind Peter was. Her mother listened gravely.

'Betty,' she said, 'does Peter remind you of anyone?'

Betty went red. 'Yes,' she said. 'You mean that he reminds you of me, Mummy? Well, you needn't worry! Now that I know how horrid it is to be with someone like that, I'm going to be different. Goodness me, I wouldn't be like Peter for anything!'

So she's trying hard. I'm glad I don't know

Peter – I wouldn't go to stay with him if I could help it, would you?

THE BOY WHO
WAS TOO CLEVER

George was a very smart boy, and always at the top of his class for everything. He thought a lot of himself, and was sure no one was cleverer than he was.

One day he went walking on Breezy Hill, and there he found a small brownie in great trouble. The brownie had got his foot down a rabbit-hole, and a naughty rabbit was holding on for all he was worth! Nothing the brownie said would make him leave go.

'Can you help me?' asked the brownie in despair, when he saw George coming along, and he told him what was happening.

'What will you give me if I help you?' asked George smartly.

'I'll give you a wish that will come true,' said the brownie.

'Good!' said George. 'Now I'll get you out of the fix you're in!'

He knelt down on the ground and began to make a noise like a fox. He barked sharply, just as a fox does in the night, and the rabbit below, holding on to the brownie's foot, heard the noise and was scared as could be! He let go the brownie's foot at once and tore away down the burrow.

'Thank you,' said the brownie gratefully. 'Now, what is your wish?'

'I wish that all the wishes I ever wish will come true,' said George.

The brownie stared at him in surprise.

'You'll be sorry for that!' he said. 'You may think you're clever to think of wishing that *all* your wishes may come true, when I've only offered you one – but you'll find you are just too clever this time!'

'Oh, no, I shan't,' said George, very pleased with himself. The brownie ran off, and George went home, thinking of all the wishes he could wish!

Well, he had a grand time! He wished for chocolate ice-cream bars, and he got them. He wished for treacle pudding at dinner-time, and he got it. He wished for a bag of toffees and a bag of chocolates, and there they were on the table beside him. Marvellous!

Then he began to feel ill because he had eaten such a lot, but he just wished he might be better, and he was! Aha! He could eat as much as he wanted, and never feel ill, because he had as many wishes as he liked. Clever George!

George had a lovely time that day. He wished for a pocketful of money, and he found shillings and sixpences and pennies jingling in his coat pocket. Then he thought he would go and buy

Lo and behold, it was in his hands!

what he liked out of the toy-shop; but when he got there he thought it would be silly to spend his money, because he could easily wish for any of the things there and have them!

'I wish for that big ship!' he said, and lo and behold, it was in his hands! 'I wish for that football,' said George, and that came flying out of the shop too, and put itself into his arms! But then a policeman came by and thought that George must have stolen the things, and he ran after him!

But George didn't run for long. He just stood still and wished that the policeman would walk the other way, and he did!

Well, for some time things went very well for George; and then one day he was walking along the river bank and he saw a little boy swimming in the water below. It was a hot day and George was puffing and blowing. He couldn't swim himself, and he was just a little bit afraid of the water. So he didn't wish to be out of his clothes and able to swim – no, he said something else!

He said, 'I wish I was that little boy and that little boy was me!'

And in a trice he found himself in the water, splashing about and swimming gaily. And on the bank stood someone looking like George, but who was really not George at all! How strange!

When George had had enough of swimming he thought he would change back to himself again; but no matter how much he wished, nothing happened! You see, he wasn't George now, he was the other little boy – and the other little boy's wishes never came true! So there was George properly caught, for nothing he could do could alter things. He had wished himself to be that boy, and that boy he was!

And what was more, that little boy was a poor little boy, with raggedy clothes, not enough to eat, and hard work to do! So George found things were very different indeed, and many and many a time he wished he hadn't been quite so clever!

'If I hadn't been so greedy over wishes I wouldn't be here now,' he thought to himself, as he ran errands all day long. 'I'd be George, a little boy with nice clothes, lots of toys, and plenty of money!'

Sometimes he heard a little laugh, and he knew who it was – it was the brownie peeping round to see how George was getting on!

'I told you so!' the brownie said with a twittering laugh: 'I told you so!'

I wonder if George will change back to himself again! I expect he will one day!

THE FAIRY IN THE CAGE

Once upon a time the Fairy Tippit felt very cold indeed. It was a frosty day and snow lay on the ground. Tippit had no overcoat and no shawl. She sat hidden in some ivy that grew up the wall of a house, and shivered.

'I really must go and warm myself somewhere,' she thought. 'There is a window just above me. If I fly up to the window-sill and peep in, I shall see if there is a fire in the room.'

So she flew up to the window-sill and peeped in. Yes – there *was* a fire there. The room was half a nursery, half a schoolroom. Toys were in a cupboard, and ink, pens, and pencils on a desk. Tippit looked at the blazing fire and longed to be near it.

'The window is open just a crack at the top,' she said to herself. 'There seems to be nobody in the room. I will fly in and get warm.'

She flew to the top of the window, squeezed in, and flew down to the floor. She looked round. The room was empty. Good! She ran to the fire and held out her tiny hands. Oh, the lovely, lovely warmth!

Tippit sat down on the cosy rug. She was

tired and the warm fire made her sleepy. Before a minute had gone by, the fairy was fast asleep. Her head rested on the fender, and her wings were neatly folded down her back.

Now the room belonged to a boy of nine. It had been his nursery and was now his school-room. His little sister Rosey used it for a nursery when she was not playing in the garden or going out for a walk. But Bobby thought of it as his own room, especially as he did lessons there every day with Miss Norris.

It was almost time for afternoon school. Miss Norris came at half-past two. Bobby had to be there first and get out his books. And so, just as Tippit was lying fast asleep on the rug, Bobby came in. The carpet was thick and his feet made no sound at all. He was just about to get out his books and slam them down on the table, when he caught sight of Tippit lying asleep by the fire.

At first he thought it was one of Rosey's dolls, and then he saw the shining wings. He set down his books softly and took a few steps towards the rug. A look of great astonishment came over his face.

'It's a fairy!' he thought. 'Yes, it really is! I've never seen one before – nor have the other children, I know. My goodness, if only I could catch her!'

He tiptoed to the toy cupboard and found an empty brick-box. He tiptoed back to the rug, stretched out his hand and snatched the sleeping fairy.

She awoke with a scream. She was held tightly in Bobby's hand and could not get away.

'Let me go, boy – let me go!' she cried in her little high voice. But Bobby grinned and shook his head. He put her into the brick-box and shut down the lid. She was caught.

Miss Norris came into the room almost at once – but Bobby didn't tell her anything about the fairy. He put the box into the toy cupboard and went to sit down at his desk. But he was so excited at the thought of having caught a real live fairy that he got his sums all wrong, and quite forgot his history lesson.

As soon as Miss Norris had gone, Bobby rushed to the cupboard. He was a bit afraid that the fairy might not have had enough air to breathe; but plenty had come through the hinges of the lid and she was quite all right, but very angry and frightened.

'If you don't let me go I shall be very unhappy,' said Tippit. 'You are not at all kind.'

It was quite true. Bobby was not a very kind little boy. He was selfish and greedy, and always wanted the best of everything for himself. His mother would not give him all the things he wanted, and he often sulked.

'I want a big green glass marble like Ronnie's,' he would say. 'I want a new hammer like George's. I want a big book of stories like

Lucy's. I want a watch like Allan's.'

'Well, you can't have any of these things until you learn to be more kind and unselfish,' said his mother firmly. 'So just forget about them, Bobby.'

But Bobby didn't forget. He worried and worried about how to get them – and now, looking at the scared fairy, he saw a way to get all the things he wanted.

'I shall make a cage for you and show you to my friends,' he told the fairy. 'Ronnie shall give me his big green marble if he wants to see you. And George shall give me his hammer. And I'll get Lucy's book and Allan's watch quite easily, because I know they'd give anything to see a fairy!'

'You are not to put me in a cage, you horrid boy!' cried Tippit, nearly in tears. 'I won't be shown like an animal at the Zoo! I won't be poked and fingered and laughed at!'

'Oh, yes, you will,' said Bobby. 'You won't be able to help it. I shan't let you go until I've got all the things I want.'

Well, Bobby set to work and made a little cage. It was a box with a piece of glass in the front, and holes at the back to let in the air. He borrowed the carpet out of the dolls' house for a rug. He took a bed from there too, and a little chair and table. He put them into the cage, and then carried the fairy there. He pushed her in, slid down the glass front – and there was Tippit, a prisoner! She could not possibly get out.

She flung herself down on the tiny bed and wept and cried. But Bobby only laughed at her. He did not care whether she was unhappy or not. Tippit said he had a heart of stone, but Bobby didn't mind what she said.

'I'm going off to tell Ronnie and George and Lucy and Allan about you,' he said. 'So wipe your eyes, tidy your hair, and make your wings neat. You look dreadful!'

'I don't care how I look,' said Tippit. 'I tell you, Bobby, I won't be shown like a lion at the Zoo. I won't! I won't!'

'Oh, yes, you will,' said Bobby. 'You can't get out of the cage – so you'll just have to put up with people staring at you.'

He ran off, and Tippit dried her eyes and thought very hard. She could not escape, that was certain. She was not strong enough to lift up the glass front of the cage. None of her friends knew where she was. Whatever could she do? She would *not* let that horrid boy Bobby get marbles and books and watches out of showing her like this.

A splendid idea came to her. Of course! Why hadn't she thought of it before? She would make herself invisible, so that she could not be seen. What a shock she would give Bobby when he came in with his friends! Ah, Bobby, what will you say then?

She muttered the magic words that made her

invisible. In a trice she had disappeared. Although she was still sitting in her chair in the cage, she could not be seen.

Meanwhile, Bobby was telling his friends about his wonderful find. They all crowded round him, excited, longing to see a real live fairy. It seemed too marvellous to be true.

'Well, you shall see her,' said Bobby, 'but you must pay me for seeing her. I've got her in a cage.'

'I've no money but you can have what you like of my toys,' said Ronnie. And the others all said the same.

'Well, give me your big marble, Ronnie,' said greedy Bobby. 'And I'll have your new hammer, George. And that book of fairy-tales, Lucy. And your watch, Allan.'

All the children were so anxious to see the fairy that they gave their things to Bobby without a word. He put the watch and the marble into his pocket, and then, carrying the hammer and the book, he led them to his house and up to the schoolroom. They all crowded in and ran to where the cage stood on the table.

'You'll see the fairy inside, either in bed or sitting on her chair,' said Bobby, putting the hammer and the book into his toy cupboard. But of course, when the children looked into the cage they could see no one at all. The rug was there and the bed and the chair and the table – but they could not see any fairy. Tippit *was* there all right, sitting on the chair, but she was quite invisible.

'There's no fairy here!' cried Ronnie.

'No – it's all a make-up of Bobby's to get our best toys from us!' cried George angrily.

'It's just a silly empty cage,' said Lucy. 'Give me back my book, Bobby.'

'And my watch,' said Allan.

Bobby ran to the cage in surprise. Sure enough, there was no fairy there! Wherever could she be? How could she have escaped?

'I'm not going to give you back your things,' said Bobby. 'The fairy is about somewhere, I'm sure. You will see her if you wait here.'

But the others did not believe him. They made such a noise that Bobby's mother came into the room.

'What is the matter?' she asked.

'Mrs White, Bobby made us all give him our best toys, and in return he said he would show us a fairy in this cage – and there isn't one!' cried Lucy.

'Bobby, how could you say a thing like that!' said his mother, who did not believe in fairies at all. 'Give back the toys at once, and go to bed for being such a naughty boy!'

Bobby had to give back the things to the others, and then, with a sulky face, he went to bed. The fairy smiled to herself. As the spell worked off she became visible again, and could be seen. She did hope no one would come into the nursery schoolroom.

Somebody did! It was Rosey, coming to put her dolls away before she went to bed. She had heard all about the cage and how angry the children were when they found no fairy in it – and as she went by the table, she peeped in.

And to her very great surprise she saw Tippit sitting there, on the little bed, looking very miserable and lonely.

'Oh! So Bobby really *did* have a fairy after all,' she said in an excited whisper. 'Oh, you dear little thing! How did Bobby catch you?'

Tippit saw the kind little face peeping in at her, and she told Rosey all that had happened. How Rosey laughed when she heard that Tippit had made herself invisible so that Bobby should not show her to the others!

'Will you open the glass front of the cage and set me free?' whispered Tippit. 'You look so kind, and I am so unhappy. I only came into this room because I was so cold.'

Rosey ran to her chest of dolls' clothes. She took out a red coat belonging to one of her dolls, and a red bonnet to match. She ran back to the cage and opened the glass front.

'Here you are, little fairy,' she whispered. 'Take these. They belong to my doll. They will keep you warm. But do, do come back and see me again. I'd so love to talk to you. I play in the garden each day, and I will come to where the crocuses grow to see if you are there.'

She saw Tippit looking very miserable and lonely

'Oh, what lovely warm clothes!' said the fairy joyfully. 'Thank you a hundred times. Yes – I will love to come and talk to you each day. And if you have any little friends as kind as yourself, tell them I will talk to them too.'

She put on the coat and bonnet and flew out of the window. Just then Nurse came in and was cross to find that Rosey hadn't put away her dolls.

'Dear, dear! what a time you are!' she said. 'What are you looking so dreamy for? Anyone would think you'd been seeing a fairy.'

'Well, I have,' said Rosey, with a chuckle. But, of course, Nurse didn't believe her, you may be sure.

And now each day Rosey sees Tippit by the crocuses at the bottom of the garden. Isn't she lucky? And Ellen, Ann, and Marjorie have seen her too. Rosey chooses somebody kind and good each day to see Tippit. Wouldn't it be lovely if she chose you too!

BOASTFUL BRENDA
AND THE BROWNIES

There was once a little girl called Brenda. She had curly hair, bright blue eyes and a very loud voice. Nobody liked her very much because she boasted all day long.

'You should see my new doll!' she would say. 'It's the finest doll in the world. It can talk and walk, and it has the loveliest dress of blue silk.'

Presently she would boast about something else – perhaps the good dinner she had had, or the new frock her mother had made for her.

'Ooh, you should have seen the treacle pudding we had for dinner! I guess it was bigger than any pudding *you* had! And goodness me, you should see my new frock! My mother made it for me and it's the best frock in town!'

Now the other boys and girls didn't like to hear such a lot of boasting. They had nice things too, but as soon as they said anything about them Brenda laughed and said she had something *much* nicer!

'She's a boaster!' said the other children. 'She does nothing but say what wonderful things she has and does. And she doesn't have anything better than we have, really. Why, she had a hole in her stocking yesterday, and the new doll she boasted about isn't even as big as Anne's old one. Brenda's a boaster! Boastful Brenda, that's what we'll call her!'

Brenda didn't know the children called her that. She just went on boasting about this, that, and the other. And one day something happened.

Brenda was walking home by herself from school one day when she met a strange-looking little man, dressed in brown and red. He was walking down the field-path towards her and they met at the stile. He stood aside for Brenda to get over and up she jumped easily and gracefully.

'You jump well,' said the little man, admiringly. That was quite enough to set Brenda boasting, of course.

'Oh, we do drill every day at school,' she said, 'and we have jumping and running, you know. I'm the best at jumping and the quickest at running. You should see me run!'

Now what Brenda said was not true – she was not the quickest at running, and although she could jump quite well, all the boys could beat her. But she badly wanted the little man to think she was wonderful.

'Dear me!' he said, 'and what else can you do?'

'Oh, I can sing like a bird,' said Brenda, 'and you should see the pictures I can draw. The teacher says they are wonderful. My writing is very good too and as for my sums, why, I can beat everybody when I try!'

'Marvellous, marvellous!' said the little red and brown man. 'Tell me some more.'

Brenda was only too ready to talk about herself. Soon she was telling the stranger all about her wonderful toy motor-car, her extraordinary clockwork clown, her fine new dress and her silver mug that her uncle had given her last birthday.

'And you should see me at home!' she ended up. 'Why, my mother and father think I'm so clever and good that they never punish me, but they listen to what I say and take my advice. They think I am wonderful.'

'Well, you're certainly a wonderful boaster,' said the little man. 'I never heard anything like it. I wish you'd come and see my family. They're the most marvellous boasters I've ever met, but I really believe you would beat them all.'

Brenda was offended. She didn't like to be told that she was boasting.

'I don't know what you mean by telling me I'm boasting,' she said crossly. 'I'm telling you the truth.'

'Oh, no, you're not,' said the red and brown man, laughing. 'You may think you are, but really you're only boasting. But you do it very well. I've never met such a good boaster.'

Brenda was just going to walk off in a temper when the little man put his hand on her arm.

'Come and see my family,' he said. 'They are the Boasting Brownies and everyone in Fairyland knows them. Do come. They live quite near.'

Well! Brenda *was* excited when she heard that fairies were near by. What an adventure to boast about to the other children. Oh, yes, she must certainly see these brownies.

'Yes, I'll come and see your family,' she said. 'But don't tell me I boast, or I'll go straight home, and I run so fast that you couldn't possibly catch me.'

'Come along then,' said the brownie, and he took Brenda's arm. He led her to a big oak tree, and pressed a little knob on the trunk. A bell rang inside the tree, and then, to Brenda's enormous surprise and delight, a small round door opened in the tree-trunk and she saw a little curling flight of steps going downwards.

'Down we go,' said the brownie, and down they went, and down and down. At last the stairs came to an end and Brenda found herself standing in a passage lighted by a swinging lantern. Big tree-roots showed up here and there, so the little girl knew she was far down below the wood.

'This way,' said the brownie, and he hurried her along the passage until they came to a small door. The brownie opened it, and to Brenda's astonishment she found herself in a very strange new world.

97

'This is Fairyland,' said the brownie, waving his hand round. 'It's always near by, but only a few people know that.'

It was a lovely place. There was sunshine everywhere. The trees were small and covered with bright flowers. The fields looked like a gay carpet, they were so well-spread with flowers – brilliant blossoms of blue and yellow that Brenda had never seen before. Little crooked houses stood here and there, and pixie-folk went about their business, their long wings spreading behind them. Some of them flew, and some of them walked. Brenda stared as if she were in a dream.

'Oh, won't the other children envy me when they hear about this!' she said.

'I don't believe you can talk without boasting, can you?' asked the brownie, curiously. 'I do wonder if you will beat my family at boasting!'

They went down a winding road, and Brenda stared in delight at the people they met. Once the brownie stopped to speak to a sandy rabbit with a red scarf round his neck, and Brenda stared at him so hard that she made him quite nervous.

'Isn't she a starer?' he said in a low voice to the brownie.

'No, she's a boaster,' said the little man. 'My, she can boast! Would you like to hear her?'

'Oh, no, thank you,' said the rabbit in a hurry, and hurried off down the road.

'I should have liked to speak to him,' said Brenda.

'Well, *he* wouldn't have liked it,' said the brownie. 'Didn't you see him run off?'

Brenda felt cross but her temper soon went as she walked on down the road with the brownie, seeing stranger and stranger sights with every step. When she saw a doll strolling along arm in arm with a teddy-bear she stood and stared in surprise, for although she had a walking doll at home, this doll seemed to be really alive.

'You mustn't stare like that,' said the brownie. 'People will think you are a starer instead of a boaster. Look, here is my house. I hope all my family are at home. They will be so pleased to see you.'

Brenda saw a queer little house, perfectly round, with an enormous amount of chimneys sticking out of the top.

'Why has it so many chimneys?' she asked in surprise. 'Surely you haven't so many fire-places in that little house?'

'Oh, no, we've only one fire-place,' said the brownie. 'But my family like to have a house with more chimneys than anyone else. It gives them something to boast about, you see.'

'It sounds silly to me,' said Brenda.

'Boasting always sounds silly,' said the little man, and Brenda couldn't think of anything to say to that. They went up the garden path and

99

the brownie opened the door, calling: 'Anyone at home?'

Three brownies, very like Brenda's friend, rushed to the doorway, all talking at once. Brenda put her hands to her ears, for the noise was dreadful. At last the noise stopped and the brownies looked at Brenda in surprise.

'Who is this?' they asked.

'It's Boastful Brenda,' said the brownie. 'I brought her because I really believe she can beat you all at boasting.'

'Oh, she couldn't do that,' said the three brownies together. 'We're the best boasters in Fairyland. We'll have a match with this little girl and see who is best!'

'Would you like a chocolate bun?' the first brownie asked Brenda. 'We made some this morning. Do sit down and make yourself at home. My name is Binks, and the other three are Tip, Cherry, and Buffle. Where are the buns?'

Tip got them from the cupboard and offered one to Brenda. She took it and bit into it.

'Quite a nice bun,' she began. 'But you should see the ginger buns my mother makes! They're lovely – so nice and hot with the ginger in them.'

'Oh, that's nothing,' said Buffle, eating a bun quickly. 'Why, I once made a ginger cake that was so hot it went off like a gun as soon as it was cut! You should have seen it!'

'I don't believe that,' said Brenda.

'What, you don't!' cried Buffle. 'Well, look here! Here's a ginger cake just like the one I was telling you about.'

To Brenda's enormous astonishment the brownie lifted up his hand and took from the empty air a big ginger cake. He set it down on the table and took up a knife.

'Now this cake is just as hot as the one I told you about,' he said. 'It will go off like a gun when I cut it.'

He cut it. BANG! It exploded in the air and a bit of ginger cake hit Brenda on the nose.

'There you are,' said Buffle proudly. 'Do you believe me now?'

'I suppose so,' said Brenda. 'Do you believe me too?'

'No, I don't,' said Buffle.

'Well, it isn't fair,' said Brenda crossly. 'You can take ginger cakes out of the air and I can't. Anyway, I know how to spell rhinoceros and hippopotamus and I'm sure *you* don't!'

'Yes, we do then!' said all the brownies at once. 'And we know how to spell Killumfhug-tonipomurath, and Fillumtrimbletigohfun-perult, and *you* don't. Ho, ho!'

'I never heard those words in my life,' said Brenda. 'I believe you made them up.'

'Well, we can spell them and you can't!' said Tip. 'You should just see all the marvellous things we can do! Why, Buffle can run like a hare. Cherry can jump right over a gate, and I can walk on my hands for half a mile!'

'I can run well too,' said Brenda, finishing up her chocolate bun. 'I can jump the best in my school, and if you showed me how to walk on my hands I could do it better than you!'

'Come on outside then, and we'll have a race!' cried Buffle. They all went out into the road and stood in a line, with Binks to give the signal for starting.

'One, two, three, off!' he cried, and away went the three brownies and Brenda. But, dear me, they ran fifty times as fast as she did, and when the race was over, how they laughed at her!

'Ho, ho! Fancy saying you could run fast! Why you couldn't race a tortoise. You're a terrible slow-coach!' cried Tip. 'Look at me walking on my hands, now! Could you do that?'

'Of course I could if I wasn't tired,' cried Brenda. 'Anyway, it's a silly thing to do when you've got feet to walk on.'

'Oh, no, it isn't,' said Tip at once. 'Because when your feet are tired, you can walk on your hands. Go on, Brenda, try it.'

But Brenda wouldn't because she knew she couldn't.

'Well, jump, then,' said Cherry. 'You said you were a wonderful jumper. What about jumping over the gate by that field over there?'

'Nobody could do that,' said Brenda. 'It's much too high.'

'I could. Look!' cried Cherry, and over he

went as light as a feather. 'Come on, Brenda, it's quite easy.'

Brenda ran at the gate and jumped, hoping that she too would rise over the gate as easily as Cherry. But of course she didn't, and down she came flat on her nose. How she howled!

'Cheer up, cheer up,' said Binks, kindly. 'You shouldn't have boasted about your jumping then Cherry wouldn't have told you to try to beat him at it. Look, you've made your nice frock all dirty.'

'It doesn't matter,' said Brenda, getting up. 'I've six new frocks at home, all new. I've more frocks than any other girl at school.'

'Ah, you haven't as many clothes as *we* have, though!' said Buffle. 'I've got twenty-eight coats, all different!'

'And I've got sixty-two hats, all the same,' said Tip.

'And I've got one hundred and two shoes, all for the left foot,' said Cherry.

'Don't tell such silly stories,' said Brenda.

'Well, come and look then,' said Buffle, and he dragged the little girl indoors again. He opened a cupboard and sure enough there were twenty-eight coats there, all different! Then in another cupboard Brenda was shown an enormous pile of hats, all exactly the same, and on a long shelf she saw scores of shoes, all for the left foot. The little girl was too surprised to say anything, though she longed to ask why all the shoes were for the same foot.

'You're not much good as a boaster really,' said Buffle. 'You're not half as good as we are. We'd better give her the Boaster's Beautiful Drink, hadn't we, brothers? That will do her a lot of good.'

Now Brenda was thirsty or she would certainly have refused to take such a strange-sounding drink. But when she saw the lovely fizzy stuff being poured into a glass, and smelt a nice orange smell, she thought she must just sip it. The sip tasted so delicious that she drank the whole glassful at once!

'You'll be sorry you did that,' said Binks, staring at her.

'Won't she be surprised!' said Buffle. 'Oh, we shall be able to boast that we made a little human girl drink our magic Boaster's Beautiful Drink!'

Brenda wished she hadn't drunk it. She decided to go home at once, and asked Binks to take her back to the hollow tree. So back they went, and Tip, Buffle, and Cherry went with them, boasting so hard all the way that Brenda couldn't get a word in!

It wasn't till the little girl was back at school that afternoon that she found out what that magic drink did! She began to boast about going to Fairyland, of course, and dear me, as soon as she spoke, a curious thing happened to her! She felt herself swelling up like a balloon! All the children cried out in surprise.

'Oh, Brenda! What's happening to you? You're blowing up like a balloon!'

Brenda stopped boasting at once, and she grew back to her own size again. She was frightened. Oh, that horrid Boaster's Drink! How dared those brownies give it to her? She sat as still as could be in the seat, doing her writing, and she didn't say another word until the teacher came round to correct what she had done.

'I haven't made a single mistake,' she boasted. 'And I didn't yesterday, either. I was the only girl who – '

Brenda stopped and looked down at herself. How dreadful! She was blowing up like a balloon again. Pop! That was one of her buttons flying off.

'Dear me, Brenda,' said the teacher, 'you are getting very fat lately. Have you been eating a lot of cream and butter at home?'

'Oh, yes,' said Brenda, at once. 'My mother always gives me cream with my porridge, and we have the best butter we can – '

She stopped again, because she was blowing up into a very big balloon-like child this time. All the other children stared with wide-open eyes. The teacher passed on to the next child and said no more. Brenda went very red and took up her pencil to write again. After a while she went down to her own size.

She was blowing up like a balloon again

106

At play-time that afternoon the children crowded round Brenda. They couldn't think what was happening to her.

'You know, Brenda,' said one of them, 'we think you *must* have been to Fairyland today, because such funny things keep happening to you – they always happen when you start boasting, don't they?'

'Yes, they do,' said Brenda humbly. 'I didn't know I boasted so much. Oh, dear, I do hope I don't swell up like a balloon every time I boast.'

'You'd be like a balloon all day long!' said a little girl, with a laugh. 'You're a dreadful boaster, Brenda!'

And very soon Brenda found out what a terrible boaster she was! She blew up like a balloon quite twelve times the next day – but after that she began to be more careful! In a week she only began to swell up about twice a day, and after that hardly at all. She had rather a bad time after her birthday, because she so badly wanted to boast of all the marvellous presents she had – but as soon as she felt herself getting like a balloon she stopped talking at once, and soon went down again.

Now she is quite cured and never boasts at all. She wants to go back and tell those Boastful Brownies that she never boasts now, but she can't find the knob on the trunk of that hollow oak tree. Isn't it a pity?

THE GIRL WHO FORGOT

Elizabeth was always getting into trouble because she wouldn't think. The things she forgot! She forgot to clean her teeth. She forgot to wipe her shoes. She even forgot to put her dress on one day and went to school in her petticoat!

It wasn't that she hadn't any brains. She had plenty – but she wouldn't use them. She simply didn't try to remember anything.

One day she was full of joy because her mother had promised to let her have a party.

'Write out your invitation cards for Wednesday of next week,' said her mother. 'You can ask ten boys and girls. You will have great fun! I will get the crackers and balloons, and you shall have plenty of iced buns and chocolate biscuits.'

The crackers came. There were three boxes, one of yellow crackers, one of red, and one of green. They did look nice. The balloons came too, and Elizabeth blew them up. They were wonderful ones, and they hung like great coloured bubbles in the dining-room, waiting for Wednesday to come.

Now, at last, Wednesday came. When she

awoke, Elizabeth remembered that it was her party, and she was pleased. But when she was scolded for forgetting to tie her shoe-laces she frowned and was cross, quite forgetting all about the party that afternoon.

'I wish you wouldn't keep scolding me, Mummy,' she said.

Her mother answered her sharply. 'Don't speak to me like that, Elizabeth. If you don't wish to be scolded, you must remember to do things properly.'

Elizabeth sulked and looked cross. Her mother was vexed and said no more, thinking that really Elizabeth should be gay and good on a party day. The little girl put on her hat and went out. It was holiday time, so there was no school. She thought she would go and see her Auntie May. So off she went.

She walked along, frowning and sulking, quite forgetting about her party. She was sulking so much that she didn't notice she had gone right past her aunt's house. So back she had to go, and didn't arrive there till nearly twelve o'clock.

'Hallo, Elizabeth!' said her aunt. 'You are just in time to go for a picnic with us. Would you like to come? I can easily tell the milkman to deliver a message to your mother, so that she will know where you are.'

'Oh, thank you, Auntie May!' cried Elizabeth, cheering up at once, and quite forgetting that of course she must go home to her party. 'I'd love to come!'

So she joined Peter and Fanny and her aunt, and they caught the bus to the primrose woods a good way away. The milkman delivered the message as he had been told, to a very astonished customer.

'Mrs Jones has asked me to tell you, Madam, that she has taken your little girl for a picnic today, and you will know she is quite safe,' said the milkman.

Mrs White stared at him. 'But it's Elizabeth's party today!' she said. 'Oh, dear – she must really come back. She must have forgotten all about it. Where did they go?'

'I don't know, Madam,' said the milkman, and went on his way whistling.

Well, Elizabeth didn't come back for the party, and all her guests arrived at three o'clock in their party frocks and ribbons. *How* surprised they were to find no Elizabeth there to greet them! Elizabeth's mother was there, of course, and she soon had the party going well, with games and balloons.

Now, in the middle of the picnic, an awful thought came into Elizabeth's mind. Surely – surely – this was the day of her party! Yes – she had waked up that morning and remembered it – and then she had been cross because her mother scolded her and had forgotten all about it!

'Auntie! Auntie!' she called in panic. 'Can I go home? It's my party today, and people are coming at three.'

'Don't be silly, Elizabeth,' said her aunt at once. 'You would surely have remembered it before, if it had been your party today. You would never have come to a picnic. You have forgotten the right day. I expect it is tomorrow or the next day.'

'No, it isn't, Auntie, really!' said Elizabeth.

'Well, your mother would have asked Peter and Fanny if it had been today,' said her aunt crossly.

'Oh, she didn't ask them because it's just my school friends this time,' said poor Elizabeth, beginning to cry. 'She's going to have another party soon for Peter and Fanny and my other cousins. Oh, do, do let me go home, Auntie May. I don't want to miss my own party.'

'Well, I am not going to spoil Peter and Fanny's picnic just because you've suddenly remembered a party that might be tomorrow, for all I know,' said Auntie May firmly. 'Here you are and here you'll stay. It will teach you to try and remember things another time, perhaps!'

So there in the woods Elizabeth stayed until it was half-past five, and the bus came by. The little girl had not enjoyed the picnic at all. She had cried all the time, and in the end Auntie May had smacked her for being so miserable.

Her Mother opened the door

She ran home as fast as she could, when she stepped out of the bus, and arrived on her doorstep at half-past six.

Her mother opened the door and looked gravely at her. 'Mummy, Mummy, what about the party?' cried poor Elizabeth.

'We have had it,' said her mother. 'We had a lovely time. All the guests are gone now. Elizabeth, how *could* you forget your own party? Everyone will laugh at you.'

'Oh, Mummy, I'll never forget things again!' wept Elizabeth, as she saw all the cracker-bits on the floor, and a burst balloon. 'I never will! Oh, I've been so unhappy ever since I remembered it was my party. Isn't there even a balloon for me?'

'Yes,' said her mother, and she gave her a pink one. 'And I kept a piece of the iced cake, a glass of lemonade, and two crackers. But you have missed the fun, Elizabeth!'

Elizabeth uses her brains now, and doesn't forget a thing! So it was a good thing it all happened, really – though poor Elizabeth doesn't think so!

HE SIMPLY
WOULDN'T BATHE!

'Charley, come and have a bathe!' shouted Alan.

'Yes, do!' said Fanny. 'It's so hot today.'

Charley was lying lazily on the rubber bed that his father and mother used on the beach, and often floated on in the water when they bathed. He shook his head.

'I don't want to bathe,' he said. 'I'm too comfy.'

'Don't be so lazy!' said George. 'You haven't even paddled today!'

'The water's cold,' said Charley.

'But the sun is so hot, and it's lovely to bathe when the water is warm in the sun,' said Lucy.

'I always think the water feels colder on a hot day than it does on a cold day,' said Charley, not moving. 'I tell you, I'm not going to bathe, and none of you can make me. So there!'

'Well, Charley, do lend us that rubber bed you're lying on,' begged Fanny. 'It is such fun to sit on it when we're bathing. We have great jokes pushing one another off.'

'I'm not going to bathe and I'm not going to lend you my floating bed,' said Charley selfishly. 'I'm going to lie here and snooze in the sun –

The waves touched the bed

and if anybody comes and annoys me I'll knock them down flat in the sand!'

That was just like Charley! He was big, and if anybody wouldn't do what he said, he just pushed them over. He was selfish too, and wouldn't lend any of his things. The children ran off, grumbling. 'It's too mean of Charley,' said Lucy. 'He knows how we all love to play with that floating bed. He's the only one of us that has one – and his mother said he could lend it to us when we bathed.'

'Oh, never mind!' said George. 'What's the use of bothering about people like Charley. He'll get his punishment one day. My mother says laziness and selfishness always bring their own reward.'

They darted into the sea, jumping high over the little waves, and having a fine time. The tide was coming in. The waves got bigger and longer, and suddenly one swept right up the sandy beach.

Lucy stopped and looked up the sand. 'Oh,' she said, 'do look at Charley! He's gone fast asleep on his rubber bed, and the sea has almost reached him. Shall we wake him?'

'No,' said Alan, with a giggle. 'He wanted his sleep and he forbade anyone to disturb him. Let him be.'

The waves touched the bed. One big one ran all round it. The next one lifted it up a little – and after that the bed was afloat!

'Oooh!' said George, 'it's floating! Look at this wave – it'll take the bed back with it!'

It did – and the bed floated neatly down the beach. The tide turned again and took the bed with it. Away on the bobbing waves went the floating bed, carrying lazy Charley with it.

The children felt a bit frightened then. They didn't want the bed to float right away, so they shouted to Charley. At the same moment a wave splashed over the bed and went on his face. He woke with a jump.

'Who's throwing water at me?' he shouted. 'I'll push you over, I'll – And then Charley saw where he was – right out to sea, bobbing on the waves.

'Come back before the water gets too deep!' yelled George. 'Come on – get back at once!'

There was nothing for Charley to do but to jump straight into the water in all his clothes and begin to walk back to the shore, dragging the bed with him. My goodness, the water felt cold! You see, Charley had been lying in the hot sun and he was as warm as new-made toast, so the water felt terribly cold.

How the children giggled when they saw Charley wading back through the sea, almost up to his shoulders in the water, looking as angry as could be!

'You had to bathe after all, Charley!' called Lucy.

'You said nobody could make you bathe if

you didn't want to – but you've had to all the same!' shouted George.

'Is the water nice and hot?' yelled Alan.

Charley's face was black as thunder. He meant to punish all the children, but when he had got back to the shore, who should come down to the beach but his mother! *How* surprised and cross she was when she saw Charley coming out of the sea with the floating bed, dressed in his shorts and jersey!

'You very naughty boy!' she cried. 'You've been bathing in your clothes – just because you were too lazy to change into your bathing-suit, I suppose! Go straight home and dry yourself, and then go to bed!'

'But, Mother –' began poor Charley. But his mother wouldn't listen to a word. She hustled him up the steps to the parade, and made him leave the floating bed behind him on the beach.

'You don't deserve to have such a nice plaything,' she scolded. 'Leave it for the other children to play with. Go along home – and mind you're in bed when I come!'

So Charley had to run home and go to bed on that lovely hot day, and the other children played with the rubber bed, and had great games with it.

'Serves him right, the lazy selfish boy!' said Lucy. 'Perhaps that will teach him a lesson.'

It did! You don't see Charley snoozing on the rubber bed any more, even when the water really *is* cold. No – he's in his bathing-suit before anyone else, and into the water he goes with a splash, dragging the rubber bed behind him. I'd like to have a game on it, wouldn't you?

'DO-AS-YOU'RE-TOLD!'

There was once a little boy called Norman, who was really a little pickle! He simply would *not* do as he was told.

If he was told to walk on the pavement, not in the road, he would walk a few steps and then slip off into the gutter again. And his mother would say, 'Do as you're told, Norman!'

If his father said to him, 'Norman, sit up straight; don't loll like that,' he would sit up for half a minute and then loll forward again. And his father would say, '*Will* you do as you're told?'

So all day long Norman heard the same thing, 'Do as you're told!' But he never did. His friends called him 'Do-as-you're-told', because that is what they always heard when they were with Norman.

'Hallo, here comes old Do-as-you're-told!' they would say. 'Come on, Do-as-you're-told. What shall we play today?'

And you may be sure that Do-as-you're-told would choose something he had been told not to do! Well, you can't go on like that for ever, and the day came when Norman got a shock.

It was a beautiful winter's day, but very, very cold. All the puddles in the road were thick ice.

The duck-pond was frozen too, and so was the village pond. The boys slid on the puddles, but they were not quite sure about the ponds. They ran to school, shouting and laughing that morning, sliding on the puddles, and gathering the white frost from the top of the posts.

When it was time to go home from morning school, their teacher spoke to them:

'No sliding on the duck-pond or the village pond yet,' he said. 'They are not safe. They may be safe tomorrow. Now, you hear me, all of you, don't you?'

'Yes, sir!' said the boys, and they trooped out into the frosty, sunny street, shouting and running.

'I say!' said Norman, as they came to the big village pond, 'look at that shining ice! It's as safe as can be! Mr Brown is wrong.'

'Now you do as you're told, old Do-as-you're-told!' laughed the boys, pulling Norman away. But he shook himself free and gazed longingly at the frozen pond.

'Wouldn't I love a good slide over the ice!' he said. 'It feels so good! Whizzzzz! And away we go, just as if we had wings on our feet. I think I'll try it and see if it's safe. I'm pretty sure it is.'

'Don't, Norman,' said the biggest boy. 'You know what Mr Brown said.'

'Well, it's too bad,' said Norman. 'I've been looking forward to sliding on this pond all the

121

morning, and now he says we're not to! That means no sliding today – and tomorrow the weather may be warmer and the ice will melt! We shall have missed our sliding!'

'Oh, come home!' said the boys. 'It's dinnertime.'

But Norman wouldn't move. He simply longed to go sliding. Silly old Mr Brown to say the pond wasn't safe! Why, the ice was as thick as could be! Norman put his foot on it to try. It didn't crack at all. He put his other foot on it, and stood with all his weight there. No cracks!

'It's safe, I tell you!' said Norman, in delight. 'Watch me slide!'

He set off over the frozen pond – he slid a lovely long way – and then, alas, he came to a thin piece! The ice cracked under his weight. It made a noise like the sound of a whip being cracked in the air.

'Oh! Oh!' cried Norman, in fright. He tried to stop himself sliding, but he couldn't. He slid on, and fell right into the water that came pouring through the cracks in the ice. He went down into the pond. It was icy cold – oh, icy, icy cold!

Poor Norman! He tried to catch hold of the sides of the ice, but it was dreadfully slippery. He yelled for help. He was wet through, and the water was the coldest he had ever felt. Even his teeth began to shiver.

The watching boys were scared. The biggest

one ran to the carpenter's shop near by, shouting for a ladder. The carpenter picked one up and ran to the pond. He placed the ladder flat down on the ice and pushed it carefully towards Norman, who was still trying to catch hold of the edges of the ice. Nearer and nearer slid the ladder, and at last it reached Norman. He caught hold of the nearest rung, and then the carpenter pulled hard at the ladder. Norman was drawn right out of the water. He began to clamber over the flat ladder, shivering and weeping.

The carpenter took him into his house, stripped off his wet clothes, and dried him in front of a big fire. Norman was very frightened indeed. He couldn't stop shivering.

'Well, Do-as-you're-told, see what's happened to you!' said the carpenter, as he rubbed Norman dry. 'I suppose you thought you knew better than Mr Brown! Now you run home in this old suit of mine and tell your mother what's happened.'

Off ran Norman, looking very queer in the kind carpenter's big suit. When his mother heard what had happened she put him straight to bed, for she was afraid he would get a bad cold.

Two of the boys came to see Norman that afternoon, after school. 'What lessons did you do?' asked Norman, sitting up in bed.

'We didn't do any,' said Harry, 'Mr Brown

He began to clamber over the flat ladder

took us up into the hills, where that old sheep-pond is. It's much colder there than here and the sheep-pond is frozen fast. We've been sliding all the afternoon! My goodness, Norman, we did have fun! You ought to have been there! The ice was as thick as could be!'

'We're going again tomorrow,' said George, the other boy. 'Perhaps you can come too, if you're all right, Norman.'

But Norman wasn't all right. He had caught a very bad cold, and his mother kept him in bed for a week. And by the time he got up, the ice had gone! The weather had turned warm, and not a single pond was frozen.

Norman was very unhappy. He had had a dreadful shock – and caught a horrid cold – and missed all the fun sliding up in the hills. He turned his face into his pillow and cried, for he felt rather small and miserable.

'I shan't disobey again,' he thought. 'Nobody punished me for it, but I punished myself, and it was a dreadful punishment!'

Now nobody calls him Do-as-you're-told. He is just as much to be trusted as the other boys. I don't expect he'll be silly again, do you?

THE STRANGE CHRISTMAS TREE

Once upon a time there was a Christmas tree that had been planted by a pixie. But before the tree had grown more than an inch or two high the pixie had gone away – so the tree grew in the wood all by itself, and didn't even know that it was a Christmas tree, for it had never been used at Christmas-time at all.

But one Christmas a woodman came by and saw the tree, which had now grown into a fine big one. The man stopped and took his spade from his shoulder.

'I could dig that tree up and sell it for a Christmas tree,' he thought. 'It would fetch two shillings at least! I'll take it to market tomorrow.'

So he dug it up, put it into a great pot, and staggered to market with it.

And to the market came a mother and her three children. They saw the tree, and the children shouted in delight.

'Mother! Buy this tree! It's the biggest and the best one here.'

So the mother bought the tree, and the woodman carried it home for her.

The tree was astonished. What in the world

was happening to it? It knew the fairy folk very well indeed, for it had lived with them for years, and knew their gentle ways and little high voices. But this world was something quite different – the people were big and tall, not like the fairy folk – and, how strange, they took trees into their houses and stood them there!

The Christmas tree didn't know that that is what we do at Christmas-time. It stood in a corner of a big room in its pot, wondering what would happen next.

The children's mother came in with boxes and boxes of toys and ornaments and candles. Soon she had hung dozens of them on the tree, and it began to sparkle and shine as if it were a magic thing. It caught sight of itself in the mirror, and how astonished it was!

'I am beautiful!' said the tree. 'I am a thing of wonder and delight! I glitter and shine. I am hung with the most beautiful things! Oh, I like living in this land, and being dressed up like this. I shall have a lovely time here!'

Now the children's mother had told them they must not even peep into the room where she had put the lovely Christmas tree. But, alas! they were spoilt and disobedient children, and they meant to see the tree as soon as their mother had gone out.

So that night they all three slipped into the room to see the tree.

'It looks nice,' said Doris.

'It's not so big as the one last year,' said George.

'It hasn't got enough toys on,' said Kenneth.

'There's something *I* mean to get, anyway!' said Doris, pointing to a box of crackers. 'So don't you ask for that, boys!'

'Don't be mean, Doris,' said George. 'You got the crackers last year. It's my turn!'

'Well, I'm going to have the soldiers,' said Kenneth, and he took hold of a box of them. 'There's only one box this year, George, and as I'm the oldest I'm going to have them. See? If you ask for them I'll smack you hard afterwards.'

'Don't be so mean and horrid!' said George. 'If you smack me, I shall smack you! I'll pinch you too!'

'Look! Look!' said Doris suddenly. 'Here's a box of chocolates. Shall we undo the lid and take some? Nobody will know.'

Now wasn't that a horrid, mean thing to do? Children that will do things like that don't deserve a lovely Christmas tree, and that's just what the tree thought. But it stood there quite still and silent, listening and looking.

The children took the chocolates – but Doris had the biggest one, so they began to quarrel again. George hit Doris, and then Doris smacked Kenneth, and soon they were all fighting. The tree was most disgusted. It had never seen such behaviour before.

The children bumped against the tree and knocked off a lovely pink glass ornament. It fell to the floor and broke.

'Silly tree!' said Doris rudely. 'Why can't you hold things properly? Why aren't you as big as last year's tree? You're not half so pretty!'

'Christmas trees are babyish things,' said Kenneth. 'I vote we ask for a bran-tub next year.'

'Yes – who wants a silly old tree now?' said George. 'We're getting too big.'

Then a noise was heard in the hall outside and the children fled, for it was their mother coming home. The tree was left alone, sad and angry. What dreadful children! How it hated staying in their house! But where could it go? It did not know its way back to the wood.

And then the tree saw four little faces pressed against the window, looking in, and heard whispering voices. It was the children of the poor woman down the lane. They had never had a Christmas tree in their lives, and nobody ever gave them Christmas presents, not even their mother, who was far too poor to give them even an orange each.

So the children had come to look at the Christmas tree in the big house.

'It's the most beautiful thing in the world!' said Ida.

'If only I could see all its candles alight and shining I would always be happy when I remembered it,' said Lucy.

'Wouldn't Mother love that box of chocolates?' said Harry.

'I wouldn't want any of those toys for myself,' said Fred. 'I'd just be happy cutting them off the tree and giving them to Mother and to you others.'

The tree listened in surprise and delight. What different children these were. If only it was in *their* home!

Then there came the noise of an opening door and the tree heard George's angry voice: 'There are some poor children peeping in our windows at our Christmas tree. Go away, you bad, naughty children. You're not to look at our tree!'

The four children ran off at once, afraid. The tree felt angrier than ever. It wanted to spank George. It shivered from top to toe at the thought of that horrid, unkind little boy! It stood there, wishing and wishing that it could leave the house.

And then suddenly it remembered some magic it had learnt from the fairy folk, and it murmured the words to itself. Its roots loosened in the pot. One big one put itself outside – and then another and another – and do you know, in a few moments, that strange Christmas tree was walking on its roots round the room! How queer it looked!

The door was open. The tree went out. The front door was shut, but the garden door was open for the cat to come in. The tree walked out of it just as the cat came in. The cat gave a scared mew and fled outside again. It wasn't used to trees walking out of a house!

The tree walked down the path and out of the gate. It saw the four children away in the distance, running to their home, in the moonlight. Slowly and softly the Christmas tree followed them. But when it got to their house the door was shut!

The tree didn't mind at all. It preferred to wait in the garden, because its roots liked the feel of the earth.

There was no front garden but there was a small one at the back. So the tree walked round and stood there in the middle. It squeezed its root-feet into the soil and held itself there firmly, a marvellous sight with all its beautiful toys and ornaments and candles.

Then it called to the fairy folk, and they came in wonder. 'Light my candles for me,' rustled the tree, 'and then knock on the children's window.'

So the little folk lighted all the candles and then rapped loudly on the children's window. Harry pulled back the curtain – and there was the tree standing in the little back garden, lighted from top to toe, shining softly and beautifully, sparkling and glittering in a wonderful way.

'Look!' shouted Harry. 'Look!' And all the

other children crowded to the window, with their mother behind them.

'A Christmas tree for us in our own garden! shouted Lucy. 'Oh, it's like the one we saw in the big house.'

Harry ran out and shouted to the others in surprise. 'It's *growing* in the ground – it's really growing! It must be magic!'

Everyone crowded round it. The tree was very happy, and glowed brightly. The children gently touched the toys. Harry cut off the box of chocolates and gave it to his mother.

And then Fred cut off the toys and pressed them into everybody's hands. He didn't want any for himself – he was so pleased to be able to give them to those he loved! But Harry made him have the box of soldiers and the red train.

Then they all went indoors out of the cold and left the Christmas tree by itself, still with its candles burning brightly. And that night the fairy folk took it back to its old place in the wood, where it grows to this day, remembering every Christmas-time how once it wore candles and ornaments and toys.

As for Doris and George and Kenneth, what do you suppose they thought when they went to have their Christmas tree and found it was gone? Only the big pot was left, and nothing else at all! How they cried! How they sobbed! But I can't help being glad that the tree walked off to the children down the lane!

DADDY'S BEST KNIFE

Daddy was very cross with Dick, because Dick had borrowed his best pocket-knife and had lost it.

'You are a naughty little boy,' said Daddy. 'First you borrow my knife without asking me – and then you are careless enough to leave it somewhere about the garden. It will get rusty and will be no use at all.'

'I've hunted for it everywhere, Daddy,' said Dick. 'I'm very, very, sorry.'

'Well, until you find my knife I forbid you to use your best toy,' said Daddy. 'Then perhaps you will learn not to lose other people's things.'

Dick looked very upset. 'Oh Daddy, my new bow and arrows are my best toy,' he said. 'Can't I play with them?'

'No, you can't,' said Daddy. 'I'm sorry, Dick, but you really must learn to be careful with things that belong to other people. You'd better hunt for that knife if you want to play with your bow and arrows.'

Dick went out to hunt again. Peter, his little brother, went with him. Dick felt sure he had looked in every single place in the garden, but he looked again.

'I had it here, when I was sharpening an arrow,' he said, standing by the garden seat. 'But the knife isn't here.'

'And you had it over there when you sharpened my pencil,' said Peter. 'But it isn't there either.'

'I simply don't know *where* it can be,' said Dick gloomily. 'It's just disappeared!'

'It's such a shame you can't play with your bow and arrows,' said Peter. 'We were having such fun, weren't we?'

'Yes,' said Dick. 'I'll have to put them away, I suppose.'

'Daddy didn't say *I* mustn't play with them,' said Peter. 'Would you let *me* play with them, Dick?'

'No,' said Dick. 'They are mine.'

'Well, couldn't I just have a turn with them?' said Peter, who really did love a bow and arrows.

'No, you can't,' said Dick. 'I don't want people to play with my things when *I'm* not allowed to.'

'Oh, Dick, you might let me!' begged Peter. 'I'd be ever so careful. I wouldn't lose a single arrow.'

Dick thought about it. He didn't want to let Peter have his bow and arrows at all. It would be horrid to see him playing with it, when he, Dick, was not allowed to.

'I really can't let you, Peter,' he said. 'You go and play with your train.'

'It's broken,' said Peter. He turned away, disappointed. Dick saw him looking unhappy, and he put out his hand and pulled him back. He was a kind-hearted boy, and he didn't like to see his brother looking miserable.

'All right, Peter, you can play with my bow and arrows,' he said. 'I won't mind. But I don't want to see you shooting. It would make me feel horrid. I shall go and read in the playroom whilst you have my bow.'

He went off. Peter was pleased to think he could have the toy he wanted, and he danced off to get the beautiful bow and arrows. Soon he was pretending to be a Red Indian and was shooting at enemies all over the place. What fun it was!

When he heard the bell ringing for dinner-time he ran to collect all the arrows. He knew there were twelve of them. He found eleven – but he couldn't seem to find the last one anywhere! Oh dear, what would Dick say if he lost one!

'I wonder if it flew up on the shed?' he thought. So he stood on the garden seat and then climbed on the shed to see. And, sure enough, the arrow was there.

And what do you think was lying beside it? Why, the knife that Dick had lost! Of course! Dick had sat up on the shed whilst he was carving a little boat yesterday. Peter remembered quite well now.

He put the knife in his pocket, scrambled off the shed with the arrow and rushed into the house. 'Dick! Dick! One of your arrows found Daddy's knife! Look! It was up on the shed!'

'Oooh, good, good, good!' said Dick delighted. 'Mother, look – here's Daddy's knife found again. Isn't it lucky?'

'Well, Dick, you got it back because you were kind enough to let Peter play with your bow and arrows!' said Mother. 'If you'd been selfish and put them away that arrow would never have found the knife for you. Kindness always comes back to you somehow.'

Dick cleaned Daddy's knife for him, and then he and Peter played Red Indians all the afternoon with the bow and arrows. They *did* have a good time, I can tell you!

RONNIE GETS A SHOCK

Ronnie was a lucky boy – I can't tell you how many toys he had! He had soldiers and trains and motorcars and books and tops and aeroplanes and everything else you can imagine. He *was* lucky.

He was something else besides lucky – he was careless! It didn't matter what time of day you went into Ronnie's playroom, it was always scattered with toys – and Ronnie trod on them as he went to and fro! He threw them into corners when he had finished playing with them. He broke them. He left them out in the rain.

'Really, Ronnie!' his mother said to him, 'You don't deserve to have such lovely toys. No sooner are they given to you than you are careless with them and break them or spoil them.'

'I don't,' said Ronnie sulkily.

'You do, Ronnie,' said his mother. 'You left that new teddy-bear out in the rain yesterday and he's a dreadful sight now – and you left your new hammer out too, and it's rusty. You trod on about twenty of your soldiers to-day and broke them. And now I see your lovely new motorcar has a wheel off!'

'I don't care!' said Ronnie.

'Be careful, Ronnie!' said his mother. 'You know the old saying, don't you? "Don't care was *made* to care!" Something may happen to make *you* care!'

'I don't care if it does,' said Ronnie.

Now, although Ronnie didn't know it, a little old witch-women called Mrs Make-you-Care was passing by the window just then. She couldn't be seen – but she saw Ronnie all right!

She had a kind face, but she could be very stern indeed. She looked in the window and nodded to herself.

'He wants a lesson,' she said, 'he wants a lesson! I'll see he gets it!'

Now that afternoon Ronnie was to go out to a party at his cousin's. He was most excited. He put on his sailor suit with long trousers. This was his party suit. He looked very nice in it – most grown up!

He went off to the party – and close behind him, quite unseen, was Mrs Make-you-Care, the little witch-woman! She trotted after him to the party – and do you know, just as Ronnie got to the door she made him ever so much smaller than he really was! He became just about the size of a doll – and in his sailor suit he looked exactly like a sailor doll!

Ronnie was astonished to find everything suddenly looking so big! He didn't know *he* had gone small, you see! He slipped in at the door when it was opened and went upstairs to the nursery, where the children were playing games at the party.

Now when he came into the room the children thought he must be a walking sailor doll that Ronnie's cousin Leslie might have had for his birthday that day! A little girl picked him up and waved him about.

'What a fine sailor doll!' she cried. 'Isn't he grand!'

And then poor Ronnie knew what had happened! Somehow or other he had been changed into a doll. He had on his sailor suit – he felt just like Ronnie to himself – but he was nothing but a doll to the others!

He didn't have time to think about it much. The children passed him from hand to hand and looked at him carefully. His cousin Leslie was surprised to see him.

'I don't remember anyone giving me a sailor doll for my birthday,' he said. 'Let's not play with him – we'll play nuts and may. That's fun!'

He took hold of poor Ronnie and threw him down into a corner. Bang! Ronnie bumped his head so hard against the wall that tears came into his eyes. He tried to get up – but he was a proper doll now and couldn't move!

He lay there watching the children playing nuts and may and musical chairs and all kinds of games. He saw them sitting down to a glorious tea, with jellies and cream-cakes and chocolate blancmange. He couldn't play games – and he couldn't eat the tea. How upset he was!

He didn't like belonging to Cousin Leslie.

'Leslie isn't kind to his toys,' thought Ronnie, quite forgetting that it was he who had taught Leslie to throw his toys about and be careless with them: 'I shan't like living here. If only I could run away! However did I become a doll? It is most peculiar. I wish I hadn't said 'Don't care' so often now!'

Nobody took any notice of him after tea. The children had a fine time hunting for presents and after that they went into the next room to see a conjurer doing clever tricks. Ronnie tried to peep round the doorway and see him too, but he couldn't.

Soon the children said goodbye and went home. Cousin Leslie ran into the nursery. He had ten minutes before bedtime. He was tired and excited.

He caught sight of the sailor doll in the corner and picked him up.

'You're a funny sort of doll!' he said. 'I don't much like your face. I don't think I want to play with you, but I'll just see if you can stand on your head.'

He stood Ronnie on his head – but of course Ronnie couldn't do that, and over he fell, bumping his knees hard. 'You're a silly doll!' said

Leslie. 'I'll stand you on your head in the inkpot!'

He opened the lid of the big inkpot and stuck Ronnie into the pot, so that his legs waved in the air, and his hair was right in the ink!

Leslie laughed and pulled him out. Poor Ronnie! His hair was black with ink and his hat was quite spoilt. Drops of ink ran down his face.

'You look dreadful now,' said Leslie and threw him down on the floor. Bump! All the breath was knocked out of Ronnie's body. He lay there and tried to get his breath back.

'What a horrid, horrid boy Leslie is,' thought Ronnie, quite forgetting that he had dipped a doll in the pond the day before! He watched Leslie looking at a book.

It wasn't long before Leslie had finished turning over the pages. He got up to get another book. Ronnie was lying on the floor just at his feet. Do you suppose Leslie stepped over Ronnie or picked him up to put him safely out of the way?

No! He trod right on top of him! Yes – as hard as he could too! Just as Ronnie had always trodden on any of *his* toys if they had been in the way!

Ronnie gave a loud squeal. Leslie looked down in surprise. 'Oh, I didn't know you were a doll that could squeak!' he said. And he trod on Ronnie again!

'Ooooooooh!' said poor Ronnie at once, because he was hurt. Leslie's foot was hard and heavy.

'What a fine noise you make!' said Leslie, and he stamped hard on Ronnie. Poor Ronnie couldn't even squeal then! He had no breath left at all.

'I suppose I've broken your squeak,' said Leslie, and he kicked Ronnie hard. Ronnie rose into the air and flew right out of the open window!

Out he went – and into the garden. Flop! He fell on to the grass lawn and lay there blinking. He felt as if he were bruised all over.

Then he heard Leslie's mother calling him to bed. 'Oh dear, oh dear!' thought Ronnie. 'I do hope Leslie remembers I'm out here on the grass! I don't want to be left out in the dark and the cold.'

Of course Leslie didn't remember to go and fetch Ronnie in. He thought Ronnie was just a sailor doll, and he didn't even think about him any more.

And so Ronnie lay out on the grass and watched the night coming. It grew darker and darker. The dew came on the grass and Ronnie felt wet and cold. And then it began to rain!

Ronnie couldn't think what the big stinging drops were that smacked him hard all over his body! They felt so very big now that he was small!

'Oh my goodness – it must be raining!' he groaned at last. 'I shall get all soft and squashy like the teddy-bear I left out in the rain the other day!'

Ronnie lay still whilst the rain wetted him from head to foot. He began to think about his own toys at home. How they must have hated it when he was so careless with them! How they must have hated him too! And now Leslie had done just the same to him!

'I wish I hadn't said, "I don't care," to mother,' said Ronnie, out loud. 'I was silly. I was horrid. Now I shall never have the chance to show I'm sorry!'

Mrs Make-you-Care was listening nearby. When she heard what Ronnie said she nodded her head. She went softly over to him and blew down his neck. Ronnie thought it was a little wind. He didn't know it was a bit of magic. He grew back to his own size again – very, very slowly, so that he didn't notice it. He was able to move! He got up and walked about. What should he do next?

'I think I'll try and find my way home,' said Ronnie. 'Perhaps my mother will know me, even though I'm a doll now.'

So, in the rain and the dark he made his way back home. The back door was open. He crept inside. He went up the stairs to find his mother. Everything seemed the right size again – but Ronnie was so tired and wet and cold that he hardly noticed it! He saw his bed standing in the corner, and he threw off his clothes and crept into it.

In two minutes he was fast asleep! And in the morning he woke up sneezing. Oh, what a dreadful cold he had got!

'Ronnie, how in the world did you get that cold?' asked his mother, surprised. 'And why is your hair so inky?'

Ronnie knew quite well – but he was much too ashamed to tell! And dear me, I'd just like you to go and see his toys now – you couldn't see a happier lot, not one of them broken or spoilt!

I don't expect he'll say, 'Don't care!' any more, do you?